# CLEAN BREAK

SQUEAKY CLEAN MYSTERIES, BOOK 15

## CHRISTY BARRITT

River Heights

# COMPLETE BOOK LIST

**Squeaky Clean Mysteries:**

#1 Hazardous Duty

Half Witted (Squeaky Clean In Between Mysteries Book 1, novella)

#2 Suspicious Minds

#2.5 It Came Upon a Midnight Crime (novella)

#3 Organized Grime

#4 Dirty Deeds

#5 The Scum of All Fears

#6 To Love, Honor and Perish

#7 Mucky Streak

#8 Foul Play

#9 Broom & Gloom

#10 Dust and Obey

#11 Thrill Squeaker

#11.5 Swept Away (novella)

#12 Cunning Attractions

#13 Cold Case: Clean Getaway

#14 Cold Case: Clean Sweep

#15 Cold Case: Clean Break

#16 Cleans to an End

While You Were Sweeping, A Riley Thomas Spinoff

**The Sierra Files:**

#1 Pounced

#2 Hunted

#3 Pranced

#4 Rattled

**The Gabby St. Claire Diaries (a Tween Mystery series):**

#1 The Curtain Call Caper

#2 The Disappearing Dog Dilemma

#3 The Bungled Bike Burglaries

**The Worst Detective Ever**

#1 Ready to Fumble

#2 Reign of Error

#3 Safety in Blunders

#4 Join the Flub

#5 Blooper Freak

#6 Flaw Abiding Citizen

#7 Gaffe Out Loud

#8 Joke and Dagger

#9 Wreck the Halls

#10 Glitch and Famous

#11 Not on My Botch

**Raven Remington**

Relentless

**Holly Anna Paladin Mysteries:**

#1 Random Acts of Murder

#2 Random Acts of Deceit

#2.5 Random Acts of Scrooge

#3 Random Acts of Malice

#4 Random Acts of Greed

#5 Random Acts of Fraud

#6 Random Acts of Outrage

#7 Random Acts of Iniquity

**Lantern Beach Mysteries**

#1 Hidden Currents

#2 Flood Watch

#3 Storm Surge

#4 Dangerous Waters

#5 Perilous Riptide

#6 Deadly Undertow

**Lantern Beach Romantic Suspense**

#1 Tides of Deception

#2 Shadow of Intrigue

#3 Storm of Doubt

#5 Bound by Mayhem

**Vanishing Ranch**
#1 Forgotten Secrets
#2 Necessary Risk
#3 Risky Ambition
#4 Deadly Intent
#5 Lethal Betrayal
#6 High Stakes Deception
#7 Fatal Vendetta
#8 Troubled Tidings
#9 Narrow Escape
#10 Desperate Rescue

**The Sidekick's Survival Guide**
#1 The Art of Eavesdropping
#2 The Perks of Meddling
#3 The Exercise of Interfering
#4 The Practice of Prying
#5 The Skill of Snooping
#6 The Craft of Being Covert

**Saltwater Cowboys**
#1 Saltwater Cowboy
#2 Breakwater Protector
#3 Cape Corral Keeper
#4 Seagrass Secrets
#5 Driftwood Danger

#6 Unwavering Security

## Beach House Mysteries
#1 The Cottage on Ghost Lane
#2 The Inn on Hanging Hill
#3 The House on Dagger Point

## School of Hard Rocks Mysteries
#1 The Treble with Murder
#2 Crime Strikes a Chord
#3 Tone Death

## Carolina Moon Series
#1 Home Before Dark
#2 Gone By Dark
#3 Wait Until Dark
#4 Light the Dark
#5 Taken By Dark

## Suburban Sleuth Mysteries:
Death of the Couch Potato's Wife

## Fog Lake Suspense:
#1 Edge of Peril
#2 Margin of Error
#3 Brink of Danger
#4 Line of Duty
#5 Legacy of Lies

#6 Secrets of Shame
#7 Refuge of Redemption

**Cape Thomas Series:**
#1 Dubiosity
#2 Disillusioned
#3 Distorted

**Standalone Romantic Mystery:**
The Good Girl

**Suspense:**
Imperfect
The Wrecking

**Sweet Christmas Novella:**
Home to Chestnut Grove

**Standalone Romantic-Suspense:**
Keeping Guard
The Last Target
Race Against Time
Ricochet
Key Witness
Lifeline
High-Stakes Holiday Reunion
Desperate Measures
Hidden Agenda

Mountain Hideaway

Dark Harbor

Shadow of Suspicion

The Baby Assignment

The Cradle Conspiracy

Trained to Defend

Mountain Survival

Dangerous Mountain Rescue

**Nonfiction:**

Characters in the Kitchen

Changed: True Stories of Finding God through Christian Music (out of print)

The Novel in Me: The Beginner's Guide to Writing and Publishing a Novel (out of print)

# CHAPTER ONE

"GABBY, I need to talk to you."

When I heard the anxiety in my best friend Sierra's tone, I braced myself. Something had happened. Something bad.

I opened the bathroom door. I'd come in from a run around the neighborhood and had taken a shower. Thankfully, I'd already gotten dressed in some jeans and a stretchy lime-green T-shirt reading, "4 out of 3 People Struggle with Math," when I heard the knock.

The water in my friend's house—which was actually a small in-law suite behind my house—had stopped working. Until it was fixed, Sierra and her family were staying with Riley and me.

Steam seeped out from behind me, along with a faint scent of lavender body wash as I dried my hair with a towel. "What's going on?"

Sierra bounced eleven-month-old Reef on her nonexistent hip. The boy reached his chubby arms toward me and babbled happily. I crossed my eyes and puffed out my cheeks. Reef giggled, drool dripping from his mouth as he stared at me.

This new stage of him being mobile was giving Sierra and Chad a run for their money. Reef was busy. And teething. And getting over an ear infection. It was the best and worst of times as a parent, apparently.

"I'm so sorry, Gabby." Sierra pushed her plastic-framed glasses up higher on her nose and frowned at me. The fact she was hesitant to tell me what happened said so much. Though motherhood had softened my friend, the animal rights activist was usually still brassy.

"Sorry for what?" I continued to towel-dry my hair, knowing I had to leave soon and that multitasking would be my only hope of getting up to Pennsylvania for an investigation on time.

Sierra grimaced. "I put Reef down for a second so I could fold some clothes. The next thing I knew, he'd toddled out of my bedroom. I went tearing down the hall looking for him and found him in your room." Her cheeks flushed.

She looked so frazzled right now. My friend was many things—passionate, focused, smart. But not usually frazzled.

"It's okay if he goes in my room." I abandoned drying my hair and draped my towel over my shoulder instead. I'd hang it in a second. My friend clearly needed my undivided attention.

"That's the thing. When I found Reef, he was standing beside your nightstand." Sierra paused, her lips pulling down in another frown—a large animated one this time.

"Okay . . ." I still wasn't sure where she was going with this, but I tried to prepare myself.

"And your wedding band was gone!" Sierra blurted, her hand flying over her mouth. "I saw your engagement ring there, so I assumed you probably took your rings off before you showered and left them. Right?"

"Yes, that's what I usually do. Did you check the floor? Reef must have knocked it off."

"I checked everywhere. It's gone, Gabby."

I scoffed. "It can't be gone. I'll move a few things around. I'm sure I'll find it somewhere."

Sierra glanced at Reef and frowned again.

That was when I understood the subtext of what she was saying. "Wait . . . you think . . . you think Reef swallowed it?"

She shrugged and pulled Reef closer. "It's the only thing I can figure."

Alarm spread through me as I realized the implications of her statement. "Is he choking? Maybe we should call 911. Or go to the ER. Or perform the Heimlich. Is there an essential oil for this?"

"No, Reef seems fine." She raised a hand to indicate I

should slow my thoughts. "There are no signs of distress."

I released my breath. "Reef couldn't swallow a ring . . . could he? His little throat can't be that big."

"Apparently, he can. It's happened before. I looked it up online after I called the doctor."

I leaned against the door. As Reef reached for me again, I planted a playful kiss on the tips of his fingers. I couldn't handle the thought of anything happening to this sweet little boy.

"What did the doctor say?"

"To keep an eye on him for any changes in behavior. Otherwise, we just have to wait for the ring to pass."

Had all of this really happened while I'd been in the shower belting out my favorite tunes from *Hamilton*?

"You mean . . ." I blinked, trying to make sure I understood exactly what Sierra was saying.

"He'll . . . you know." Sierra grimaced before shrugging sheepishly. "We should find it in his diaper in a day or two. But the doctor gave me a whole list of things to look out for, just in case it doesn't pass as expected."

"I don't know what to say. But I'm seeing a certain theme in my life lately."

I knew it was uncouth to say, but that theme was . . . excrement.

I didn't like it any more than anyone else, but it was the truth.

First, I'd been introduced to the most delicious coffee

ever. I'd later found out it was made from cat poop. Then I found out the argan oil I used in my hair was made from . . . what else? A fruit that was first eaten by tree-climbing goats and then defecated. Now my wedding ring would pass through the valley, so to speak.

What was God trying to teach me? That sometimes the best things in life came after a big stink? That you had to dig through a lot of muck to find the gold? That it was possible to find beauty in unexpected places?

As I looked at Reef, I knew I couldn't be mad. "I'm just glad he's okay. I'm thankful it was my wedding band and not my engagement ring."

"Me too. I'm so sorry, Gabby. I'll make this up to you . . . somehow."

"Don't worry about it. I'm going out of town for a couple days. When I get back, I'll return to being an old, married woman, right?" The doctor had made it sound like it would be that easy.

Sierra nodded, but her trembling hands showed she was still nervous. "Let's hope."

"This too shall pass." I cringed over my word choice, but Sierra didn't seem to notice.

I glanced at the bathroom counter where I'd left my phone. I had a meeting in six hours. However, I had a five-hour drive to get there. Because of a tight schedule, I couldn't be late.

"I've got to get moving." I made one more silly face

at Reef and held it until he giggled. "Keep me updated on this little guy. I'm sure he'll be fine."

She pushed her glasses up again, uncertainty still hovering in her gaze. "Thanks. I hope so."

The location of my wedding band was the least of my concerns right now.

My immediate priority was helping an old friend find some closure in her life . . .

So far, there had been no gold at the end of her less-than-pleasant situation. I was determined to remedy that.

Spring was blooming late this year. It was April, but everything was just now beginning to turn green again after a chilly winter. As I headed north on the desolate road along Virginia's Eastern Shore, my phone rang.

I smiled when I saw the number. Riley.

I hit Talk on my Bluetooth. "Hey, babe. How are you?"

"Sorry I missed you before I left." His deep voice rumbled across the line. "Court took longer than I expected. You ready for this new case?"

"As ready as I can be."

I hated to sound like a downer, but my Cold Case Squad had already done a bunch of investigating online, which had yielded nothing. We'd had no choice but to meet up in Pennsylvania and investigate our latest case in person.

I'd been on the road a lot lately, traveling all over the region doing workshops for Grayson Tech. Through my bread-and-butter job, I taught law enforcement officials how to use various equipment at crime scenes. I only worked the Cold Case Squad on the side.

Coffee mogul Garrett Mercer had started and now funded the Cold Case Squad. Computer nerd Sherman MacDonald and cool but brilliant psychologist Evie Manson were my colleagues. We were on our third case together. Some might not even consider our current investigation a cold case, but all the leads had dried up.

We were looking for Angela Vance, the foster mom Evie grew up with. Angela had disappeared six weeks ago, and no one had heard from her since.

Though none of us were cops, we'd be doing some good, old-fashioned police work by hitting the streets and talking to people in an effort to find information we couldn't gather online.

I hoped we'd find some answers. But I could already feel that this case was going to be challenging.

"I'll be praying for you guys. I know this means a lot to Evie."

"Thank you." I took a sip of my coffee. The Americano with heavy cream and sugar had become one of my road trip essentials.

The fact that the case was personal, in some ways,

made it even harder. So much was riding on finding these answers. Without closure, I wasn't sure Evie would ever be the same.

"It's probably good timing that you're working on this case now," Riley said. "Work is keeping me busy this week."

Riley's career as an attorney had been very demanding lately. I bit back a frown.

Neither of us loved how much time our work took us away from each other. In fact, Riley had mentioned a few times that he desired to start his own law firm again.

I'd also been feeling restless lately, but I figured this was just the stage of life we were in. I chided myself for feeling that way. I supposed it could be, in part, due to the fact that every time things began going well in my life, a big catastrophe struck. Coincidence? Maybe.

But life experience had taught me to be aware.

Just then, my phone beeped. I glanced at the number. It was my boss, Margo Grayson. "I should probably take this."

I said goodbye to Riley and switched over to hear Margo's voice on the line. "Gabby, I hope I'm not catching you at a bad time."

Something about the way she sounded put me on edge. Her voice was too stiff and formal for our usual easygoing, professional relationship.

"I always have time for you," I told her, hating the fact I sounded like a kiss-up.

"I don't want to beat around the bush, Gabby. I respect you too much for that."

My body instantly tensed—just as it had when Sierra knocked on my bathroom door earlier. "What's going on?"

"I wanted to let you know that Grayson Tech has been bought out by Titov Industries."

I sat up straighter, unsure if I'd heard her correctly. "What? What does that mean?"

"It means you will no longer have a job."

# CHAPTER
## TWO

"I DON'T UNDERSTAND . . ." I pulled the car over to the side of the road so I could process what Margo had just told me. The company was doing so well. Why sell out? Why did this mean my job was eliminated?

"This new company . . . they're forcing us to cut about 60 percent of our work force. They want to bring in their own people. It's not entirely unusual in these kinds of situations. I realize this is upsetting for you."

Upsetting was an understatement. This would change my life. "How much more time do I have?"

"A month. We're making the official announcement tomorrow."

I leaned back in my seat, trying to process that. One month. That didn't leave me much time to find a new job. It could take months to go through the search, interview, and hiring process . . .

I was overthinking this. Still, worries came at me like Nazis searching for the von Trapps in *The Sound of Music*.

"Are you okay, Gabby?" Margo asked.

"I don't know how to answer that."

"You're bright, and you've got initiative. I know you'll find another job, Gabby. Just look at all the connections you've made throughout your time working for me."

It was true. I did have a lot of great contacts, thanks to my job with Grayson. But contacts didn't equal a paycheck. Even though Garrett Mercer funded these Cold Case Squad investigations, all of us did this on the side—it wasn't a full-time gig.

"Thanks for your vote of confidence." My voice sounded strained.

"I'll be happy to provide you with a reference. Whatever I can do."

"Thanks." As I ended the call, all I could think about was how I was going to tell Riley.

Because this had been the last thing I'd expected today, and I wasn't sure what this would mean for his dream of starting his own law firm.

---

I was the first to arrive in Shady Valley, Pennsylvania. The little town was located only twenty minutes from what was commonly referred to as Amish Country—the Lancaster area. My colleagues and I had rented three rooms at a bed-and-breakfast, where we would be surrounded by rolling acres dotted with cows and horses, fields plowed like quilt patterns, and a strange nothingness that vaguely reminded me of the movie *The Village*.

The house itself was an old farmhouse with three floors and six bedrooms. Helene lived on the first floor, and guests stayed on the second and third floors. The place wasn't especially well-decorated, but it was clean and felt as welcoming as a mother's hug. It was perfect for us.

I checked in, deposited my luggage upstairs, and chatted with the innkeeper, Helene Brown. I learned that she was a widow, she'd owned this place for five years, and she loved to bake.

The woman was tall and painfully thin, with salt-and-pepper hair pulled back into a tight bun. She told me she'd grown up Amish but had left the community in order to marry Tom, who'd been "English," as the Amish referred to outsiders.

She still had hints of her upbringing—she wore only dresses and no makeup, and nothing in the home seemed frivolous. I found the simplicity refreshing.

As I waited for the rest of the gang to arrive, I sat in a little sunroom facing the back of the property. A few stray chickens foraged on the wide lawn, and a small, rustic building stood off to the side with ivy growing over the peeling paint. A pasture stretched out back, and a side road, empty of traffic, ran alongside the property.

Freshly squeezed lemonade waited on a crocheted tablecloth in front of me, along with a plate of oatmeal cookies. A cool spring breeze swept through the open window. I ignored the vague scent of manure, choosing to call it fresh air instead. The scent was in no way related to the life lessons God seemed trying to teach me lately.

Evie and Sherman were going to share a rental car from the airport, and I expected them within the next fifteen minutes.

Until then, I decided to review my case notes.

Forty-nine-year-old Angela Vance hadn't been seen in more than six weeks. For many years, she'd been a foster mom. She had no biological children of her own. After her husband left her four years ago, she stopped fostering and decided to go back to college and get a degree in teaching.

I stared at her picture, which I'd also slipped into my file. Angela was pretty in an understated kind of way. She could almost pass for Evie's biological mother since they were both thin and had dark hair. In this photo, she wore a Georgetown sweatshirt and jeans. The Baltimore harbor stretched behind her.

Several months ago, Angela signed up for an online dating site. My colleagues and I had thought the last man she went out with was named Ed Wilson. We discovered we were wrong. In February, Angela had come here to Shady Valley to meet a guy who used the alias Bob Linder.

It was the last time she was ever seen. Local police had given up on finding her. We had no explanation for her not contacting Evie all this time. They'd been close.

Sherman knew his way around a computer better than Hammerstein knew his way around a musical. But there was no web footprint to be found for her since that day. We'd talked to the dating website, done internet searches, made phone calls. And we'd only reached dead ends. Evie was typically cool and self-controlled, but I could tell that she was troubled by the lack of communication.

We hoped by coming here and talking to people we might discover something new.

I heard tires squealing outside. I paused and glanced out the window.

A beat-up white truck sped down the road, revving its engine. The sound seemed so out of place here in the serene setting. I continued to watch as a man extended his arm out the passenger window and tossed something into the yard.

I sucked in a breath.

Was that a . . . Molotov cocktail?

I rushed to my feet when I saw the flames on the grass.

# CHAPTER
# THREE

I DARTED into the kitchen and grabbed a fire extinguisher from the wall. Then I sprinted outside, determined to put the blaze out before it spread.

As I reached the small fire, another man darted from an outbuilding on the property. He grabbed a hose and began spraying the flames.

I squeezed the nozzle on the fire extinguisher, watching as foam covered the grass and the orange flares disappeared. Finally, the last flame was extinguished, leaving puddles on the small plot of charred grass.

I hauled in a deep breath, my adrenaline still pumping. That had been unexpected.

The man cut the water spray and let out a long sigh before shaking his head. He was probably in his sixties and stout, with a receding hairline. His rounded features made him seem homegrown and down-to-earth, as did his well-worn jeans, flannel shirt, and work boots.

"That wasn't how I wanted to spend my afternoon," he muttered.

"We need to call the police. I didn't get the license number of the truck, but I can describe the vehicle." I paused to cough. More smoke had gotten into my lungs than I thought.

"Won't matter." He dropped the hose and shrugged, acting as if things like this happened every day. "The police won't do anything."

What did *that* mean? "Who was that? Why would they do something like this?"

"Just trying to be a nuisance."

"A nuisance? This whole place could have gone up in flames." His statement seemed a little lackluster.

"They knew I'd get out here and put it out. That's why they threw it here, far enough away from the house that I'd have time. Besides, the grass is still a bit damp from the rain early this morning."

He made all of this sound so routine. Shouldn't he be more upset?

Before I could ask any other questions, the man extended his hand. "I'm George, by the way. I apologize for the lack of hospitality."

"I'm Gabby. I'm staying at the bed-and-breakfast." The conversation seemed too mundane after what had just happened. My heart still pumped harder than a fire hose.

"I live back here in the guest house. Helene is my sister-in-law, and I stay around to help her out as needed. Mostly, I take care of the horses. We have ten."

I wasn't sure if the fire could have spread quickly enough for this whole place to go up in flames or not. But I did know that fire wasn't something to be played with. It seemed anticlimactic to simply continue on with life as if nothing had happened.

"Are you sure you don't want to call someone?" I asked.

George shrugged. "It's taken care of. Fire's out. End of story."

I was going to have to take his word for it. I wasn't a country girl, but maybe people preferred to handle situations like this themselves out here.

George ran a hand over his face, as if he were exhausted, and he started to roll up the hose. He was obviously putting this incident behind him. "What brings you out to this area?"

"I'm actually here to investigate the disappearance of a woman."

George raised his eyebrows. "Is that right? Sounds fascinating. I hope you're able to find this lady. I feel the need to warn you, though. People in this town—they're not always welcoming to strangers."

They didn't seem too welcoming to residents either

if someone could set a property on fire in broad daylight. His words caused a knot to form in my stomach. First, he'd mentioned he didn't trust the police, and now this . . . "What do you mean?"

As the words left my mouth, I wondered if the man who'd thrown the Molotov cocktail was connected in some way with our presence here.

It should have been out of the question, but I'd seen stranger things happen before. However, no one in town should know we were here—no one except Helene and now George.

George frowned and ran a hand over his face again. "Unfortunately, my sister-in-law and I have made some enemies in the area."

Enemies? Helene had seemed as sweet as apple pie. Not the kind of person someone would dislike, let alone try to torch.

Would my friends and I be safe here? Maybe we should find another place to stay. This wasn't a prank—grown men tried to set this place on fire. What did they have in mind next, and did we want to be in the middle of it? George seemed so calm that I felt I was overreacting.

"Like I said, people around here, they don't like outsiders." George roped the hose around his shoulder and took a step back. "Anyway, I'll let you get back to what you're doing. Thanks again for your help. Don't worry too much about this. It's more of an empty threat.

Believe me. I've been around the block a few times with these guys."

I had only taken a step away when I heard him call me again, and I paused.

He stood where I'd left him, a wrinkle on his forehead. He remained quiet a moment before asking, "Do you take on other cases?"

"What do you have in mind?"

"There's someone I've been looking for also. It's not Laurie Sparks you're here about, is it?"

"No, I'm sorry. It's not."

He frowned. "She just kind of disappeared off the face of the earth about two years ago. If you would take the case, I can see what I can scrounge up to pay you."

Something about the way he said the words tugged at my heartstrings. Maybe I would help him. I didn't know. I didn't have much time here, but maybe I could take the case later, especially now that I was losing my job.

"Get the information for me, and I'll see what I can do," I finally said. "While I'm here in town, I'll be concentrating on this case, but maybe I can help somehow."

George offered a sad smile. "Thank you. I appreciate that."

Suddenly, my stay here seemed awfully full. I knew we didn't have much time, and I wondered how everything was going to play out.

The one thing I knew for certain was this: we had to find Angela.

Evie needed closure. I knew from personal experience just how tough it was to be left with only questions, and I didn't want anyone else to experience that heartache.

Not if I could help it.

---

As I walked back into the bed-and-breakfast, Evie and Sherman entered the sunroom, suitcases at their sides, and stared at me as if I'd lost my mind. I supposed I *was* a mess. For all I knew, I could have soot on my face or fire-tinged hair. It wouldn't be the first time I'd looked like a drowned scarecrow.

"Did you just put out a fire?" Sherman squinted through his thick glasses at the fire extinguisher in my hand. He rubbed his squarish face and blinked as if my appearance had totally thrown him off-kilter.

"You smell like smoke," Evie echoed, shaking her long, straight hair and scrunching up her thin nose in disgust. She was a MENSA member and forensic psychologist, so I didn't bother to answer the obvious.

They must have just pulled up out front and effectively missed the excitement out back.

Before they could say anything else, I interjected with, "It's a long story."

Evie eyeballed me. "It's always a long story with you, isn't it?"

I wanted to argue or be insulted at her typical socially awkward question, but I couldn't be. She was absolutely correct. Still, I pretended I didn't hear her and moved on.

She seemed cold as ice and was difficult to love, but I loved her anyway.

Sherman was in love with Evie in a different way, but she was clueless about his romantic feelings—and she thought marriage was archaic. I still hoped she'd soften enough to allow herself to be open to finding happiness. But that remained to be seen.

"I'm so glad both of you made it here." I squeezed Sherman's arm and nodded at Evie. She didn't welcome physical touch.

Evie glanced around with a disapproving frown. "Wherever here is."

My friend would never win any awards for a bright and sunny disposition. Just because she was a city girl didn't mean country living was inferior. I had a feeling her biggest challenge would be living without Starbucks and high-speed internet.

"Did you check in?" I asked.

"There was a note on the door," Evie said. "I guess the innkeeper had to run to the store."

That would explain why Helene hadn't come out during all the excitement.

I tried to put the fire out of my mind so I could lead this meeting. But being a taskmaster wasn't a part of my natural skill set, unlike turning everyday situations into musicals or mentally snarking at people.

"You guys ready to get started?" I asked.

"We've been ready." Evie gave me duck lips. She'd mastered them long before they were cool.

"Let me go change first," I said. "Give me a second."

I was back downstairs less than five minutes later, and we all sat at the table in the sunroom. Sherman poured a glass of fresh lemonade for Evie and then one for himself. I pulled out my dossier, the one I'd taken so much pride in making for our meeting. I'd already sent copies to Evie and Sherman so we could maximize our time here.

I tried to keep my thoughts focused on the mystery at hand. But my adrenaline still pumped from putting out that fire, from hearing about how unfriendly this town was, and realizing I wouldn't have a job in a month.

"I feel bad that Garrett is using his resources on this." Evie's pale skin looked even paler than usual against her black blouse. It hadn't been long since I'd last seen her, but something seemed even more broken and hollow than it had before. She might never ever admit it, but the disappearance of the only woman she'd known as a mother had taken its toll on her.

I gripped the case file in my hands. "This is your life,

Evie. This case is important to us, just as important—if not more—as any stranger's cold case."

"I know, but—"

"No buts about it." Sherman shifted his stocky frame in the white wicker chair. "This is what we all agreed to come here and do."

I swallowed hard. "Okay. Let's recap what we know. Unfortunately, we don't have a ton to go on here. Angela's cell phone went dead on the day she went missing. None of her personal belongings, like a purse or wallet, have shown up anywhere. We know Angela and Bob met at a restaurant here. There are only six in town, so it shouldn't take too long to visit those places."

"I've called all those restaurants in the past, and no one remembered anything." Evie raised her eyebrows, looking defeated before we even began.

"But maybe coming here and talking to people face-to-face and showing her photo will help," I said. "We can also talk to the police."

"I've already talked to them as well. They seemed about as incompetent as they come. They didn't care, and I don't think they'll be any help." Evie rolled her eyes.

It was really hard for me to be the grown-up of the group, the one who remained cool and collected even when emotions flared. But I was determined to be the best version of myself.

Yep. I'd been reading a book on that very subject.

Listening to some podcasts. The old Gabby was a thing of the past. This new Gabby was poised. She resisted saying the first thing that came to mind. She was . . . well, kind of boring, truth be told. But I was trying to be mature, like any good adult would be.

"I Won't Grow Up" from *Peter Pan* began playing in my mind. The song seemed to taunt me whenever I took strides forward.

I might act more mature, but I secretly still liked snark and flip-flops and quoting my favorite songs at the most inopportune times. Some things would never change.

Case in point: my sarcastic lime-green T-shirt was hidden beneath my professional blazer.

"Someone here has to know something. We just need to find that person." I glanced back and forth between my two friends, waiting for their response.

"I still think we should consider the idea that Angela just walked away from her life," Evie said. "It wouldn't be the first time this has ever happened to me."

"Even if that did happen, we should be able to find her," Sherman said.

"Maybe she left just like my foster dad did." Bitterness tinged Evie's words. She certainly wasn't going to make this easy.

"You know her." Sherman's voice softened. "You know she wouldn't do that to you."

"I don't know anything," Evie said. "Everyone I've ever depended on has let me down."

"Not us," Sherman insisted.

"There's still time." Evie crossed her arms.

I straightened my papers and kept my voice even as I said, "We're doing our best here, Evie. I promise we are. We want answers."

She nodded stiffly. "I just don't want to get my hopes up. I'm sorry for being snappy. This is . . . it's hard. I could discover answers that I don't want to know. It goes against everything I've ever learned, but maybe it's better if I believe the lies I'm telling myself instead."

There it was. The truth and a brief moment of vulnerability. I felt invisible pressure to say the right thing. But what was the right thing?

I cleared my throat. "If you know the truth, you can move on."

"Let's hope." She let out a breath, seeming to break out of her doldrums a little. "Okay, I say we get started. Shall we divide and conquer?"

"It's not a bad idea since we have limited time," I said. "Let's make like a pea and split."

Evie gave me a look.

And suddenly it felt like old times.

# CHAPTER
# FOUR

I PULLED my blazer closer as I paced down the sidewalk of downtown Shady Valley. Irritation pressed on my chest.

Not only had my visits to two different restaurants been unsuccessful, but no one I'd talked to seemed interested in helping. They barely even glanced at the photo of Angela. George was right. This town wasn't welcoming.

I might as well be Harold Hill going back to River City after people figured out his con game. The residents I'd talked to had given me the shortest answers possible, hadn't smiled, and seemed anxious for me to leave.

I was meeting Sherman and Evie back at a little municipal park located on the edge of town so we could share what we'd learned. I hoped they'd had more luck than I had.

As I headed down Main Street, I noted how cute the town itself was. Main Street was lined with old buildings that held hints of grandeur. Many of them looked like they'd been untouched for years. A hardware store sign looked circa 1960. Everything was still in place—the name, the window displays, the handwritten hours. But the building itself appeared abandoned.

From what I'd read online, when the railroad had stopped using the tracks running through the area back in the eighties, business in town had dried up. Now everything was a shell of what it had once been.

I shoved my hands more deeply into my pockets as my thoughts shifted. The one thing that was certain in life was change. There was no doubt about that.

In one month, I would no longer have a job. I still couldn't believe it. Working for Grayson Tech had been an answer to prayer. The position had been only part-time, but it paid well. The job had allowed me to do some PI work on the side, to train law enforcement professionals, and to make great contacts.

What was I going to do now? Did I want to dive full-time into PI work? I didn't think so.

But, if I didn't do that, then what? I certainly didn't want to go back to crime-scene cleaning. Besides, I'd sold my business to Chad.

The weight on my shoulders seemed even heavier.

Sometimes life liked to knock you on your butt. This was one of those times. I'd risen above the muck before, and I would do it again. I just had to figure out a way to break the news to Riley.

I paused when I reached the corner. My gaze scanned everything around me.

No one else was out on these sidewalks.

Then why did I feel like I was being watched?

An eerie sensation shimmied up my spine.

I didn't know why I felt this way. I only knew it was never a good sign.

At that moment, a man on a motorcycle zoomed by. I couldn't make out many details about the rider. But his head turned toward me, making it clear he'd seen me. That he was watching. That I didn't belong.

No, I clearly wasn't welcome here. And that was going to make our job ten times harder.

---

A few minutes later, I arrived at Valley View Park. The place had a small playground, several picnic benches, and a happy little brook that cut through the center. Beyond the foliage that surrounded the area, I spotted the tops of several houses.

In the distance, a mom pushed a young boy on the swing. Otherwise the park was unoccupied. It was nearly dinnertime, so perhaps most people were at home right now.

I met my cohorts on the sidewalk that wrapped around the perimeter of the area.

Based on Sherman and Evie's expressions, they hadn't had any more luck than I had.

"Nothing." Evie crossed her arms, her black leather coat stretching across her thin shoulders.

"Same here," Sherman added with an apologetic shrug.

"And nothing here either." I frowned. "Not only had no one seen anything, no one seemed interested in helping us."

"I noticed that." Sherman pushed up his glasses. "Everyone just looks tense, like they resent us being here. It's really strange, like we stepped onto the pages of *Wayward Pines* or something. I've never actually experienced it in real life before, though."

I wasn't ready to give up. Someone somewhere saw something. We just had to find that person.

"You're here to investigate?"

I turned my head toward the voice. An older woman stepped from behind a tree. No, not from behind a tree. She'd been walking down a little trail that appeared to cut through from the park to a neighborhood.

Evie, Sherman, and I exchanged a glance before looking back at the woman. She was probably in her eighties and hunched over with a cane—but otherwise, she seemed to get around just fine. Her white hair was short and curled, her glasses were thick, and her mint-green winter coat oversized for her slight frame.

"Yes, we're here to investigate," I finally said. "Do you know something about Angela Vance?"

"Angela Vance?" She squinted before shaking her head. "No. I can't say I do. But that other woman who died here last month. I thought you were talking about her."

"Another woman?" I questioned, my curiosity sufficiently spiked. "Who was that?"

"No one knows her name. She was found strangled right here in this park." Using her cane, she pointed to a patchy area of grass.

My hair rose, and I glanced around. This place seemed so peaceful with its trickling brook, rocky hillside, and cheerful play area.

But things weren't always as they seemed. Just what was this town hiding?

# CHAPTER
# FIVE

EVIE STEPPED CLOSER to the woman, her gaze narrowing with intensity. "What did this unnamed woman look like?"

The woman shrugged. "She was young. In her early twenties. Blonde hair. Thin."

I released my breath. That didn't fit the description of Angela. Thank goodness.

Evie chomped down, as if she was at a loss for words. Maybe any kind of answer was better than living with the unknown. I didn't know.

"I'm sorry to hear about what happened here." My voice cracked as I said the words. "Unfortunately, that's not the case we're investigating."

The woman grunted and continued to shuffle forward. "Would sure be nice to know what happened to her. Might help us all sleep better around here at night—but don't tell anyone I said that."

The woman pushing the boy on the swing turned and waved. "Grandma!"

"If you'll excuse me," the woman muttered. "If anyone asks, we never talked."

As quickly as the woman appeared, she was gone.

I turned back to my friends. What did that mean? *Don't tell anyone I said that. If anyone asks, we never talked.* Was she just a crazy woman stirring up trouble?

"A murder? That's . . . disturbing." I'd always wanted to think that small towns like this were peaceful. But no place was immune to crime. I wondered about the woman George had asked me to look for. Was she from this area also? I needed to ask him. "Anyone hear anything else about a murder before you came here?"

"I didn't," Sherman said. "Which is weird. I did investigate this town. You would think that would have come up, right?"

"Right." Crime usually shook small communities.

"We can't get distracted here." Evie's gaze cut into mine. "We're here to find Angela. We don't have time to get sidetracked."

"Of course. That's our first priority." I squared my shoulders. "I still want to talk to the police."

"They're not helpful," Evie reminded me, raising one of her thin eyebrows.

"I know. But I want to give it a shot. How about you two go and see if there are any cameras around town that might help us? You know the drill. Look at ATM machines, traffic lights, parking lots. If we can find the cameras, maybe we can find the footage."

Sherman put his hand on Evie's elbow. "That sounds great."

He could sense her dark mood also, couldn't he? It almost seemed like she was working against us.

I'd been there before during some hard periods in my own life. There was no way to know how things would turn out. You just had to pray that you'd be strong enough either way.

With a final nod, I took off toward the police station. I prayed for Evie's sake that this trip wouldn't be in vain. I also prayed the answers wouldn't devastate her.

---

The police station was located in a stand-alone building two blocks over from Main Street. It was a simple brick structure with ten parking spaces out front. Three official police vehicles were parked there.

After walking through the front door, I paused.

Only three seconds in, and I already knew why Evie had a bad impression of the place.

The front desk was unoccupied. A plant died in the

corner. Christmas decorations had been left on a table in between chairs in the waiting area.

I'd been in plenty of police departments around the region in my job with Grayson Technologies. But something about this place felt dead.

I pulled myself together, stepped up to the desk, and pressed on a little bell there.

I resisted the urge to tap my finger on the countertop, even though my patience was waning. No one could hear me over the TV, which sat on a little desk in the corner, just barely within eyesight. A basketball game blared.

Stepping toward the side for a better look, I clearly saw two officers there, feet propped on their desks, gazes fixated on the screen.

This town had no hope if these two were in charge of monitoring the criminal activity. They couldn't even monitor their station. Irritation rose in me.

Though I'd told myself I was going to be a grown-up and I tried to visualize myself as a professional, something instinctual took hold inside me. I crossed behind the counter, grabbed the cord to the TV, and jerked the plug from the wall.

The room went silent.

The officer closest to me lurched to his feet and stared at me with a look in his eyes that clearly said I'd just crossed boundaries like a cat strutting through a dog pound.

"Excuse me?" He practically spit the words out. "Who do you think you are?"

I stared at the man. Early thirties. Dark, wavy hair. Stocky build. Eighties-style mustache that was so thick it looked like a wooly worm had taken up residence above his lips. His name badge read "Chief Cruiser."

The other officer still remained at his desk, watching our exchange. He looked edgy, as if he might jump into action given the right signal.

"I tried ringing the bell, but no one heard me." I used my sweetest voice, adding a slight Southern drawl. "I just stood there and rang it and rang it. I didn't know how else I could get your attention."

Chief Cruiser's shoulders softened. "Sorry. I guess the TV might have been loud. But strangers shouldn't come in here and touch things not belonging to them. Now what can I do to help you?"

I tilted my head. Body language 101. Tilted heads looked innocent.

"Someone I know was supposed to come to this area for dinner. She disappeared, though, and now I'm real worried about her. I'm really hoping you guys can help."

Appeal to their masculine sensibilities while seeming clueless was an effective technique I'd learned through the school of hard knocks.

"Who is this friend of yours?" The chief shifted his weight, his puckered expression conveying annoyance.

"Her name is Angela Vance." I pulled a picture from my pocket. "I'm really concerned that something happened."

He glanced at the photo. I watched for a sign that she was familiar. After all, Evie had been in touch with the police. The chief should have seen this picture before. But I didn't see even a flicker of recognition there.

Interesting.

"I haven't seen her." He looked back at me, the photo already forgotten.

"Exactly. That's kind of my point." My words came out sharper than I wanted, so I let out a little laugh and tilted my head again. "I mean, no one has seen her. I reckon that's why I need your help."

He stared at me, a good dose of skepticism in his eyes still. "What do you want us to do?"

Had he really just asked that? "File a Missing Person's report. Look into her disappearance maybe. I don't know . . . I just need you to help, to make sure nothing bad happened to her." It took entirely too much effort to keep my voice calm and unassuming. I didn't have to fake looking worried—I *was* worried about her.

Chief Cruiser exchanged a look with the other officer. Something about it made me uncomfortable, but I couldn't pinpoint what exactly.

Finally, he leaned toward me, drawing his words out slowly. "Ma'am, have you ever considered that maybe she never came here? That maybe she escaped a life she didn't want anymore and just disappeared—on purpose?"

Irritation burned inside me. Any professional worth his salt would ask more questions before coming up with these theories. He hadn't even heard enough information to begin piecing that together.

I leaned against the counter and kept myself in check before saying softly, "You don't know Angela. She wouldn't do that. She had people who mattered to her."

"Maybe they mattered too much. Maybe they were too much of a burden. Maybe they were the reason she ran."

Okay, this guy was a jerk.

I unfisted my hand before I punched him in his arrogant jaw. "Angela wouldn't do that. No one has seen or heard from her in more than a month. Something is wrong. You've got to believe me," I added with a little whine to my voice.

Chief Cruiser shrugged again. "I'm sorry. There's nothing we can do to help you. If there's no sign of foul play, then there's no crime and nothing to investigate."

I swallowed back a terse reply and purposefully widened my eyes. "But you're the police. If you can't help me, who can?"

He shrugged yet again. "Sometimes you've just got to help yourself, lady."

With that, he plugged the TV back in, went back to his seat, and propped his feet up on the desk.

He was in for a surprise. Because when people dismissed me, that only made me more determined to prove them wrong.

# CHAPTER
# SIX

I STEPPED out of the police station and onto the sidewalk, anger snaking through my muscles until I felt viperish all over. That man didn't deserve to wear the name of law enforcement official.

But Chief Cruiser the Big Time Loser had encouraged me to look into Angela's disappearance on my own, so that was exactly what I planned to do.

If I wasn't on a time crunch, I might investigate this town. Between what had happened earlier at the bed-and-breakfast, our cold reception, and the generally eerie sense I got, this town deserved to be profiled just like a serial killer might be.

I paused there on the sidewalk and felt my hair rise again. My internal radar was finely tuned from years of sticking my nose where I shouldn't.

I scanned the area but didn't see anyone watching me—though I definitely felt eyes on me again.

Then two men walked across the street. They leered at me.

Strange.

Farther down the sidewalk, a family of four strolled back toward an SUV parked on the street. Their glances also remained on me for a little too long.

Also strange.

Why were these people all looking at me like that?

I didn't know, and I didn't like it.

"Hey," someone called.

I snapped from my thoughts and turned to see Sherman and Evie rounding the corner. Sherman held up his phone, where he'd no doubt been taking photos. He was a tech guy who didn't believe in pen and paper —not when you could either take a screenshot or a picture.

"We found a couple cameras," he said. "I'm going to go back to the bed-and-breakfast and see if I can find out how to access them. It will be a good starting place, at least."

We knew no one would give us permission to look at their security cameras. But Sherman was an expert at getting into digital places that were otherwise off limits. I assumed it was slightly illegal, but I avoided learning the laws regarding technology so I could plead ignorance if confronted.

Occasionally, investigating demanded subterfuge—fake identities, cover stories, creative ways of finding out information. The laws were meant to protect the innocent from being taken advantage of, and that's exactly what we were doing when we gathered information. Every case I took, I prayed I would do the right thing.

I nodded. "That sounds good."

Progress sounded good. I reminded myself we were just getting started. I couldn't expect a lead to simply fall into our laps like pollen on a spring day.

Evie stared at me and tapped her boot against the cement. "What about you? What did you find out?"

I remembered my experience in the police station and narrowed my eyes. "You were right. Police here are no help at all."

"It's embarrassing, really, isn't it?" She shook her head, as if disgusted. She should be. Officials like that were an embarrassment to police officers everywhere.

I let out a long breath. "Listen, how about if we grab some dinner, talk things over, and then go back to the bed-and-breakfast. Sound like a plan?"

My stomach rumbled, reminding me that I needed to eat. I'd grabbed a quick sandwich on the way here, but that ham and cheese was long gone—kind of like our leads.

Evie, Sherman, and I sat at one of the little restaurants I'd visited earlier today. Pumpernickels was located on Main Street in what used to be a house, and it smelled like sauerkraut and sausage. Some people might not like the scent, but it had my stomach rumbling with anticipation.

The downstairs had been turned into an eating area. The walls around us were all brick, the ceiling low, and the lighting dark. I'd never been to a German pub, but this place looked what I imagined one would be like with its shiny wood and thick furniture.

We'd ordered drinks—water for me—as well as some onion rings as an appetizer. The waitress wasn't particularly friendly. I'd talked to her earlier when I came in, but now she barely showed any recognition. She simply did her job and scurried away.

Evie reached into her pocket, unfolded a paper, and smoothed it out on the table. She cleared her throat before saying, "I put together this timeline. It really isn't much help, which is why I didn't show it to you earlier. There are so many holes in Angela's schedule it could double as a watering can. Maybe we can fill some in."

I twisted my neck so I could better see the paper.

Friday, February 11: Meets Bob online, per Sherman's research.

Saturday and Sunday, February 12–13: Friends said everything appeared normal. Emails confirm she set up the date with Bob in Shady Valley. Rest of the conversations between Bob and Angela must have taken place on the phone. No online record of it.

Monday, February 14: Talked to Evie on the phone. Didn't mention her date.

Tuesday, February 15: According to neighbors, Angela left her house at 3:30 p.m. If she'd come straight here, she should have arrived around 5:30.

That was the last time anyone heard from her.

As I stared at the timeline, our appetizer came. I grabbed an onion ring and tore it in half. Steam seeped out. I dipped the deep-fried goodness into some horseradish sauce and let the spicy flavor wash over my taste buds.

"Okay, you said her credit cards haven't been used." I snapped back to the present, ignoring "Old Town Road," which played on the overhead and beckoned me to sing along while mentally doing a FortNite dance my ten-year-old neighbor had taught me.

"That's correct," Evie said. "There's been no activity on them since that Tuesday when Angela stopped once to get gas."

"So we know for certain she was on her way here. Sherman, have you talked to this Bob Linder guy?" I glanced at him as he played hot potato with an onion ring, tossing it from one hand to the other.

"All I know is that he was using an alias," Sherman

said, giving up and placing the deep-fried vegetable on a napkin. Grease spread across the paper like an oil spill in the Atlantic. "I managed to get into the online dating website Angela and Bob were using. He used a prepaid credit card, so we can't trace his financials that way. We do have a picture, but who's to say he used his own?"

"So how else can we track this guy?" I asked. "There has to be another way. Fake name, fake picture, untraceable credit card. But he has to have an IP address where his messages came from, right?"

"I'm working on it," Sherman said. "It's not always as easy as the movies make it seem."

"It never is." I leaned back, irritated at myself for feeling so stumped. We'd just started this investigation, and I already felt like it was drying up. Usually, I had a good idea where to start. "I feel like we're missing something, like there's something obvious we should be looking into but aren't. No one just disappears."

"I think our best bet right now is to check out the camera footage—if we can find any," Sherman said. "A lot of places only keep the recordings for a few days or a week. It's been six weeks now."

"What about her car?" I asked, glancing at Evie. Was that the piece of missing information I'd been searching for? "Where is it now?"

"It hasn't turned up. It was an older model, so it didn't have any kind of GPS or tracking capabilities. I found an insurance card at her place with the VIN on it and put a notice out, but nothing has turned up."

We had only three days here in Shady Valley. Three days to figure out what happened to Angela. Three days to find answers so Evie could put her mind at ease.

I had a feeling this could be one of our toughest cases yet—in one of the toughest environments.

# CHAPTER
# SEVEN

"SO, HOW'S IT GOING?" Riley's voice rolled across the line.

Even after nearly a year of marriage, I still felt a shiver of delight when I talked to him. I knew I'd found my soulmate when I met him, and I was so thankful that the bumpy, twisted path to love had ended with Riley and me together.

I stood at the open window of my room at the bed-and-breakfast, a cool breeze floating inside. I could hear dry grass rustling with the wind, hear the faint neigh of horses, and sense a country stillness. This was officially the best part of my day.

It wasn't yet dark outside, but the sun was beginning to set, casting pastel-colored light over the landscape. With a sunset this pretty, the town itself couldn't be that bad, right?

"This whole case has been tricky," I told him, crossing an arm over my chest. "There's not much evidence to go on. Without evidence, it's hard to know which direction to go to find answers."

"How about witnesses?"

"That's the other thing. No one here in this town seems to have seen Angela. Even the police department doesn't seem to care or even be vaguely interested."

"That's unfortunate, to say the least."

"How do we even figure out who this guy is that Angela was supposed to meet? Riley, I'm telling you— I've never felt so stumped, and I've done a lot of official and unofficial investigations." I closed my eyes and let the breeze wash over my face. It almost felt like a kiss from God above.

"Maybe trace some of the other women this guy was communicating with. Maybe one of them can ID him— or tell you something that would help."

I straightened. "You know what—that's a great idea."

"I have a few of them sometimes."

As a moment of silence fell, I realized this would be a great time to tell him I lost the job with Grayson. I just didn't want to. I mean, he'd been talking about quitting the firm where he was working. Said it was taking up too much of his time.

But if I lost my job, then he wouldn't be able to afford to do that.

I was going to crush his plans for the future.

I opened my mouth, and I found myself asking, "Did Sierra tell you about Reef?"

"And your wedding ring? Yes, she did. Sierra was very upset by it all."

"I just want Reef to be okay. Has he . . . passed it yet?"

"No, not yet. Just be glad you don't have the job of finding it after he does."

I grimaced at the thought. "I am. Very glad."

He paused before saying in a hoarse voice, "I miss you, Gabby."

My heart melted a little.

"I miss you too, Riley. I love you, and I'll see you in a couple of days."

"Okay, sounds good. Good night."

"Tell Sir Watson I said goodnight also."

"The dog's been moping since you left."

"Just show him one of Sierra's cats," I said. "He'll perk right up."

"You're terrible."

"Terrible? No. I love cats."

"No, you don't." He chuckled.

My heart still felt warm and gooey as I ended the call and pressed the phone to my chest.

But I had to tell him the truth. And I would. Tomorrow.

I closed my eyes for just another moment. When I

opened them, something in the distance caught my attention.

My eyes widened when I saw Helene's horses racing across the pasture.

I swerved my gaze toward the other side of the fenced-in area.

The gate was open.

What?

I didn't know much about farm life, but I knew if those horses got out, it was going to be a headache to round them up again. And that was the best-case scenario. Worst-case scenario? They'd run into the road and keep running, putting them in danger and potentially causing an accident.

Just as the thought entered my mind, the horses ran from the fenced-in pasture onto the road.

I had to do something. Now.

⁂

I tore down the stairs so quickly that I heard Evie and Sherman's doors open behind me.

"Where's the fire?" Evie muttered.

I ignored her and kept going. I almost went to Helene, but, instead, I bypassed her room and tore out the back door. I hoped my eyes hadn't been deceiving me. That gate had been open, and at least six horses had run through it.

I didn't know enough about horses to know how to rein them in without getting trampled myself. I'd seen a small house in the distance earlier. Right now, yellow light glowed in the windows.

My feet pounded up the front porch, and my fist slammed into the door. Only a couple seconds passed before it opened, and George stood there.

"What in tarnation—"

"The horses got out." My voice sounded raspy as I sucked in air.

He raised his head, as if unsure he'd heard correctly. "The horses?"

I nodded. "I just saw them run out the gate."

He jerked his boots on and ran from his house to his truck.

"Come on," he called. "I'm going to need your help."

I didn't ask any questions. I climbed into his late model Ford F-150, and we took off down the gravel lane toward the road.

"How long has it been?" George hunched over, his gaze scanning the road in front of us.

"Just a few minutes."

He grunted again. I wasn't sure what the grunt meant, but I had a feeling it wasn't good.

I looked at the seat between us and sucked in a sharp breath.

A gun lay there.

Who had I just gotten into this truck with?

# CHAPTER
# EIGHT

"GIRL, why do you look frightened? Haven't you ever seen a pistol before?"

"Yes, but usually only when people wanted to kill me."

"What?" He threw me a confused glance. "We're in the country. Everyone out here carries them."

He probably had a point. My life experiences had tainted me. Too many guns had been pointed at me, accompanied by threats.

"There they are!" I pointed to the horses. They ran down the road at full speed.

George's foot hit the accelerator. "I have to cut them off before they reach the highway."

"How did they get out?"

"Your guess is as good as mine." He raced down the road.

I closed my eyes, hardly able to stand watching. I felt George veer to the side of the road and then throw on the brakes.

Only after we'd been stopped for several seconds did I open my eyes.

The horses had stopped and now stared at us.

Before I could ask questions, George climbed from the truck and began muttering something to the animals. But his gruff words were undercut by the affectionate way he rubbed each horse's nose.

He opened my door and tossed me his keys. "Follow behind us. I'm going to lead them back."

I didn't argue. Instead, I scrambled out of the truck and around to the driver's seat. I watched as George put a lead around one of the horses, probably the alpha. The rest of the horses began following behind.

Moving slowly, I remained a good distance behind George. It was nearly magical the way they all followed him, never straying off the path.

I was just glad they were okay.

Now, if we could say the same for Angela.

---

"What happened?" Evie rushed toward me as I climbed out of the truck. She tightened the sweater around her neck, and her hair had been pulled back into a sloppy ponytail.

I explained to her what had transpired. My adrenaline still pumped. Who knew a day on the farm could do that to a person? But it had.

"Wow." She frowned and stared off into the pasture. "I'm glad you saw it when you did."

"Me too." I glanced behind her, wondering why she was out here alone. "Where's Sherman?"

"Helene looked like she might pass out. He stayed inside with her."

"He's a nice guy," I said. Maybe one day Evie would get the hint and see that the best thing to ever happen to her was right in front of her.

Well, not me. I was officially the one in front of her. But Sherman. Inside the house. You know what I meant.

Evie shrugged. "I don't think anyone can argue that Sherman is nice."

I frowned. She didn't think his kindness was a big deal. But it was. I only wished Evie could see just how special Sherman was.

My gaze shifted back to George as he worked out in the pasture. He took each of the horses into the stable, where he was probably securing them in their stalls for the night. Several minutes later, he strode back outside and toward me.

"Thanks for your help." He let out a long breath, the circles under his eyes looking bigger, deeper.

I handed him his truck keys. "No problem. Any idea what happened?"

He let out a long breath. "My best guess is that someone opened the gate and then did something to spook the horses."

"Why would they do that?" Evie blinked, as if perplexed by such a simple-minded act of mischief.

"Someone has been picking on Helene for a while now."

"Picking on her?" Evie repeated, her eyes widening. "I'd call that Molotov cocktail a little more than picking on her. Someone could have gotten hurt."

"They were just trying to send a message," George said. "Believe me, I know how these guys think."

Evie shrugged. "If you say so. I think I'd be moving out if someone did that to me."

"Then they'd get what they wanted."

"Why do they want her out of here so badly?" I asked.

"Helene bought this property. It used to belong to the Cruiser family, but it went into foreclosure. They want it back."

"They sound like bullies," Sherman said.

"Tell me about it." George shook his head. "Anyway, it's one of the reasons I moved in here. To give her a hand after my brother, Tom, died. I've never been married myself, so it only made sense that I help."

There was obviously a lot more to this story than I'd assumed. Was this connected to the fire earlier today?

"Anyway, that's why I came here. Helene needed help. She couldn't run this farm by herself."

"I guess not. But what do you mean by someone has been picking on her? What else happened?"

"Just strange, little incidents that keep occurring. Things like the gate being left open. Water left running and driving up the bill. An absurd number of nails in farm vehicle tires. And, of course, there was the little surprise someone threw into our yard today."

"You think someone is trying to sabotage her?" I asked. "Why would someone do that?"

George's jaw tightened. "She's . . . well, not just Helene. Both of us are newcomers here. Sometimes, towns don't like new people. That's all I can say."

"But—" I wanted more information.

"Anyway, thanks again for your help. I need to go check on Helene. I take it you both can see yourselves back in."

"Of course." I crossed my arms as I watched him disappear into the house. Then I turned to Evie. "I don't like the sound of whatever's going on here."

"Me neither. It's like this whole place is shrouded in mystery."

"Yes, it is."

With one more glance back at the stables, I released my breath. There was no need to stand and think about this too long. I hadn't seen anyone out here tampering with anything. There might be footprints on the ground, but there had been too many people in this area to distinguish one set of prints from another. Without the right resources, those tracks would do me no good.

I'd think about it more tomorrow.

In the meantime, I glanced at my watch.

It was only seven. I still had some time to work. I needed to make the most of every minute.

---

Two hours later, Sherman had been able to find the names of three other women who'd been in contact with Bob Linder. First thing tomorrow morning, I was going to call them.

Until then, I pulled my laptop onto my legs. I typed "Dead woman Shady Valley" into my search engine. I held my breath, waiting to see what results populated the screen.

I knew our focus was on Angela Vance, but I couldn't help but be curious about this other murder the grandmother at the park had mentioned. It seemed foolish not to at least do a quick sweep over the facts of what had happened.

To my surprise, hardly anything came up online about her. How was that possible? In a small town like this, a dead body would be the talk of the community for weeks—if not years—to come. It didn't make sense.

I broadened my search to the surrounding area and

finally found a small snippet about the death in one of the larger newspapers from Lancaster County.

"An unidentified woman believed to be in her early twenties was found dead in a municipal park in Shady Valley," I read. "The blonde was approximately 120 pounds with blue eyes. The only identifiable marker on her was a gold necklace with a rose pendant. Police have no suspects but encourage anyone with information to call . . ."

It appeared no one had called. At least, there were no follow-up stories.

Wasn't someone's life worth more than one inch of column space in the newspaper? Why was no one advocating for this woman?

I felt the fire igniting inside me, but I tried to hold it back. I had no proof or any reason to believe this Jane Doe was in any way connected with Angela Vance's disappearance. But I couldn't stop thinking about her.

My to-do list for tomorrow kept growing longer and longer. There were too many loose ends—ends that flapped teasingly in the wind, nearly taunting me.

And I hated being taunted.

# CHAPTER
# NINE

THE NICE PART about staying at the bed-and-breakfast was that breakfast was included. Helene really knew how to cook. Homemade biscuits sat in a basket at the center of the table, and each plate had eggs, bacon, and hash browns. The orange juice was freshly squeezed, and the coffee smelled heavenly.

I didn't eat like this every morning, but, while I was here, I was going to enjoy this indulgence. When I closed my eyes, the scent of smoky bacon made my stomach growl with pleasure.

Evie, Sherman, and I were the only guests at the moment.

Helene stood by, watching over us like a dutiful hostess as we dug in. Though I did wish for some privacy so I could talk to my friends, I understood that this wasn't the time or place to get that privacy.

As I took another sip of coffee, Helene bustled over to refill my cup.

I also had questions for her about what had been happening, but it didn't seem the right time to ask.

"So, it seems the three of you have made quite the stir in town." Helene stepped back and took her place in the doorway.

Her words stopped me mid-bite of my buttered biscuit. I lowered it back onto my plate. "Is that right?"

Had news traveled that fast?

"I don't pay much attention to gossip, but three people like you going around and asking questions . . . well, it has people talking. I thought I should let you know." Helene didn't seem to take delight in the words. Instead, she looked burdened by them with her mellow voice and subdued actions.

"You almost say that as if it's a bad thing." What was the subtext of her comment? I wasn't sure, but it almost sounded like a warning.

"People don't always take well to strangers here." Something flickered in her gaze.

Were there really still towns like this in America? I mean, I saw them on TV, but I rarely experienced them. I thought they were a dramatic novelty taken for entertainment purposes. "Really?"

Helene began to absently straighten some teacups on a cart in the corner. "This town and its residents . . . most of them go back for generations. There's really no industry here. A lot of people are farmers. Some people travel an hour or so to get to work. There are a few attorneys or other town workers who are strictly local. But it's a closed community. Very untrusting of outsiders."

Did that explain all the strange looks I got yesterday?

"What do you know about the cops here?" Evie asked, looking unaffected by Helene's words. Instead, she spread some strawberry jam on her biscuit, every motion prim and proper.

Helene paused, seeming more comfortable with that question. "Duncan Cruiser is the current chief. His dad was chief before him. Hardly any crime here, except for the occasional speeder. Locals here believe that if there is crime, outsiders must be responsible."

I remembered the dead woman in Shady Valley Park. Remembered the man in the truck who had thrown that Molotov cocktail. How did they justify those things?

Or was a local responsible, and was the police chief trying to protect someone?

I didn't like the thought of it.

I realized Helene could be a great source of help and information to us. She had just the insight we needed, and her loyalty didn't seem to be with the town.

"Are you an insider?" I began picking at my biscuit again as I waited for her answer.

She let out an airy laugh. "Well, no. I live on the

outskirts of town, obviously. This land came up for sale, and my husband and I bought it. We just wanted to get away and needed some place to start fresh. This seemed perfect at the time, but we didn't really know the area as well as we thought."

In other words, she was an outsider also. I wondered about her story. About the courage it must have taken to leave everything and everyone behind for love and a new start.

"Do you mind if I throw another question at you, Helene?" I asked.

She glanced down at her hands. "No, of course not. I'll answer if I can."

"Yesterday, we heard about an unidentified woman who was found dead at a park in town more than a month ago. Do you know anything about her?"

Evie nudged me under the table. I'd explain myself to her later. I had my reasons for asking, and she had her reasons she wanted me to leave it alone. But what if Angela's disappearance and this woman's death were connected?

Helene's skin paled, and she swallowed hard. "I did hear about that, mostly through the town scuttlebutt. It's a tragedy, isn't it?"

"It is. I'm just surprised there wasn't more about it in the news."

"No one made a big deal about it." Helene shook her head. "It kind of surprised me, but George says that it's just because there was so little evidence about what happened to her."

So little evidence . . . that seemed to be a theme around here.

"I imagine everyone in town was scared," I continued, popping another piece of biscuit in my mouth. "I mean, a dead body? That shakes people up usually."

"You'd think people would be scared, right? But everyone just seemed to continue on, trying to mind their own business."

"Strange." Weren't people curious? Frightened?

Her eyes met mine and understanding passed between us. "Yes, very strange."

I wanted to ask her questions about last night. But I stopped myself. I had only two days here. I couldn't wrap myself up in but so many mysteries.

But curiosity burned inside me.

---

Evie, Sherman, and I finished breakfast and then escaped to the sunroom again for our morning debrief. I hoped we would make some good progress today. I hated the fact that we didn't have much time to figure this out. Then, again, sometimes the time crunch pushed us to move faster, to work harder.

I couldn't wait to share a few things I'd learned last night. I hoped they had something to share with me also. So we could have a visual, I pulled up a picture of the supposed Bob Linder on my phone. He was a middle-aged man with a large forehead, close-set eyes, and small lips. He was no supermodel, but his eyes looked warm.

I held up my phone so my colleagues could see his photo.

"So, get this," I started. "I made some calls this morning before breakfast to some of the other women this Bob Linder guy had been out with—thanks to the information Sherman gave me. They all said the same thing about him. That he seemed nice enough but kind of boring. Unassuming."

"Just like Ted Bundy," Evie added drily.

I ignored her. "Most of them had very little helpful information. However, one of them actually saw this guy's car—and his license plate number."

Evie straightened. "Really? Did she remember it?"

"She did. I'm running it right now and hope to have some results ASAP."

"That's good news, at least."

Sherman raised a finger. "I also have an update. I was up for most of the night trying to tap into some of those security systems and camera feeds that Evie and I found. Most were a bust—their footage from that time period had been recorded over. But I did have one hit."

I waited as he pulled up something on his computer and turned the screen to face us.

"It's grainy, but I think that's Angela walking down the sidewalk here in Shady Valley. The timestamp indicates this was taken the day she came here to meet Bob. What do you think?"

I leaned closer for a better look. He replayed the scene. Sure enough, that looked like Angela Vance strolling down the street. But that wasn't Bob with her.

No, it was a woman wearing a knit hat and a bulky coat.

# CHAPTER
# TEN

"I FEEL like I've seen that woman," I muttered, freezing the screen.

"Me too." Evie leaned closer.

"It's one of the waitresses from the restaurant last night." Sherman grinned, proving he'd just been waiting for us to come to the same realization. "She's not the one who waited on us, but she worked the other side of the room."

Excitement surged in me. "That's right. I didn't talk to her yesterday, only to the manager. We need to talk to this lady. She might be the only one who had the answers we needed."

Evie's gaze met mine. "Yes, we do need to talk to her."

My phone dinged, and I glanced at the screen. "I've got a match on that license plate. The car belongs to someone named Robert Murphy. He's from Reading, which is about an hour from here."

"Sounds like we've got two leads." Sherman sat up straighter. "Which one do we pursue first?"

I glanced at my watch. "Pumpernickels doesn't open until lunch. I think we should head to Reading. Try to find Robert. By the time we get back here, the restaurant will be open and we can track down the waitress. What do you think?"

"Sounds like a plan. Besides, it's not like anyone is going to offer up any information on where we can find this waitress. Catching her at the restaurant is our best bet." Evie rolled her eyes. "This town is backward."

"It gives me the chills." I couldn't even argue with her. Instead, I stood. "Okay, I'm ready to go. How about you two?"

Evie and Sherman both rose also. But before we could step from the room, Sherman's phone beeped. He paused and glanced at the screen. A huge smile spread across his face.

I watched him, wondering what in the world would make him grin like that.

He typed something back, still staring at the screen.

Evie's eyes narrowed, and she tapped her foot impatiently. "Sherman?"

"One second," he murmured. He continued to type, continued to grin.

Wait . . . there was only one reason he would smile

like that. Was he texting someone? To another woman? Maybe even a girlfriend?

That had to be it.

But . . . I glanced at Evie. I thought Sherman was in love with Evie. Had he decided to move on?

Finally he cleared his throat, put his phone away, and turned back to us. "Sorry about that."

"Who were you texting?" Evie narrowed her eyes with suspicion.

"No one important." He shrugged, but his face turned red.

"People don't usually grin like that over people who aren't important." Evie wasn't going to let this drop.

"It's just . . . a coworker. A new coworker."

"A female coworker?" I asked, unable to stop myself.

He blushed and shrugged again. "She is a female, yes. I was assigned as her mentor at work, so we've been talking quite a bit."

I glanced at Evie and saw her let out a little harrumph. Was she jealous? I couldn't be sure. I certainly wasn't going to ask. But maybe some competition was just what Evie needed to realize Sherman was perfect for her.

"Daylight's burning." Evie squared her shoulders. "Let's hit the road."

The hills on the drive to Reading were beautiful with their rocky outcroppings mixed with large stretches of green grass. We passed several Amish buggies and numerous farms. For a moment, I felt like I'd been swept away into another world—this one more welcoming than Shady Valley.

The area truly was beautiful.

It was too bad we were here for reasons other than enjoying the scenery around us.

I could tell Evie was nervous. She was quiet, staring out the window as she drove their rental car. There were no visible signs of her nerves. But, despite that, I could sense them.

This was hard on her.

"Turn here." Sherman pointed to a road up ahead.

Evie followed his directions and pulled into a neighborhood. I hoped this was it. I hoped we could track down this Robert guy and finally get some answers.

A moment later, we pulled up to a dark blue bungalow. It definitely wasn't anything fancy. The outside was neat with low-maintenance flower beds and short grass.

A well-used silver sedan was parked in the driveway.

The license plate matched the vehicle we were looking for.

Did that mean Robert was actually home right now? Could we be that lucky?

After a look at Evie and Sherman, we all climbed

out. The chilly breeze seemed to warn us to go away, but I ignored it.

"I think I should take the lead here," I started, expecting Evie to argue with me.

She didn't.

As a psychologist, she understood that her emotional involvement in this case could make her a liability. I made the most sense.

Wiping my sweaty palms on my jeans, I climbed onto the tiny porch and rang the doorbell. Then we waited.

I heard movement inside the house.

Someone was definitely home.

But no one was answering.

That usually meant one thing.

"Stay here," I muttered.

With my friends guarding the front door, I scurried toward the backyard. Just as I opened the gate, I spotted someone darting through the grass.

It was a man. He was running.

And I couldn't let him get away.

# CHAPTER
# ELEVEN

"HEY!" I yelled before taking off toward the man.

He looked over his shoulder and sped up. He had just enough of a head start that I feared for a moment I wouldn't catch him.

Just as he tried to climb the privacy fence and throw his leg over, I grabbed his belt. With one jerk, he fell to the ground. He moaned as his body hit the grass.

"Over here, guys!" I yelled. I quickly glanced back toward them, making sure no more trouble had shown up.

In the brief second I looked away, the man sprang to his feet. He scrambled toward the fence again, this time easily throwing himself over.

"You've got to be kidding me . . ."

I sprinted after him, climbing the fence, and landing

with surprising gracefulness on the other side. That didn't happen often.

I pulled myself up to full height and scanned the new area. Another yard.

I spotted the guy near the gate.

I couldn't let him get away.

I sprinted toward him, my long legs more nimble than his.

He opened the gate and glanced back. As he did, I tackled him.

He hit the ground with a thud. I landed on him with another thud.

But this time, I wasn't going to let go.

"You have some explaining to do, Robert," I growled, staring the man down. I pulled myself up on my knees and turned him over. I wanted to see his face, his eyes.

"You can call me Bob." He flinched, as if he feared I might sock him in the face.

It might be tempting but unnecessary. I lowered my hand but remained straddled on top of him so he couldn't move. The man looked just like his picture. Dark hair with a touch of curl. Rounded nose and jaw that gave him a chubbier appearance than necessary. Wide, fearful eyes.

Evie and Sherman caught up with us and stood on either side of me, their breathing heavy with exertion.

"What did you do to my mom?" Evie barked, standing over us.

I hadn't expected that voice to come out of her. For a second, I considered putting myself between her and Bob, fearing she might attack the man. But I'd give it some time first. She was usually pretty levelheaded.

"Your . . . your mo—mom?" Bob practically stuttered the words out.

As his gaze flittered around anxiously, I couldn't help but think he looked frightened. Nonthreatening. Not at all like a criminal.

But I couldn't make any assumptions here.

"Angela Vance." Evie glared down at him. "What did you do to her?"

"I didn't . . . I didn't do any—anything to her. Why would you think I did?" Sweat sprinkled his forehead.

"Because I haven't seen her or heard from her since your date with her," Evie shot back.

"Wait . . . you think I hurt her?" His eyes widened. "Why would I do that?"

"You were probably the last person who saw her," I said. "You're not using your real last name or location. What are you hiding, Bob?"

He flinched. "I'm not hiding anything. I'm just terrible at dating."

"We're going to need more than that, Bob." I glared at him, still holding onto my bad cop routine. He had ticked me off, so it wasn't a stretch.

"I don't know what you want me to say. I would never hurt her."

"You're going to need to tell us more than that if we're going to believe you," I said before adding, "Bob."

I put a lot of emphasis on his name. For some reason, I found it very satisfying to say it with every sentence I directed at him.

"Okay, okay, okay!" He raised his hands. "I can explain. We were supposed to meet. That's true. But . . . I didn't actually meet her."

"What do you mean?" Evie still leaned over him, her foot still dangerously close to his hand and inching closer by the moment.

"I mean, I chickened out." He flinched and jerked his arm from the ground.

Evie must have stepped on him.

I gave her a dirty look, but she either didn't see me or ignored me.

Bob wrung his hands together, his breaths coming faster. "I have this thing. My mom always said I was afraid of girls. I always told her that wasn't true. But, honestly, maybe it is. I break out in hives when I think about talking to an attractive woman face-to-face. I've never really even had a girlfriend, and I'm nearly fifty."

"Keep going."

"It's why I turned to online dating. I felt like I could be myself. It seemed like women actually liked me when we chatted on those message boards. I thought maybe I could gain some confidence."

I took everything he said with a grain of salt. "Why use a fake name?"

"I was afraid they would figure out who I really was. They'd know I was a fraud. I don't know. I realize that sounds crazy. But, to me, Robert Murphy is equated with a socially awkward loser that people would rather make fun of."

I didn't want to feel sorry for him, but I did. Or, at least, I was starting to. "What about your credit card then? Why use a prepaid one?"

"I don't believe in credit cards." He shrugged. "My mom taught me not to go into debt. That included credit cards. I bought this house with cash. Bought my car with cash. I know I need a card sometimes for online purchases. Whenever I need those, I preload one of those credit cards I can get at the gas station. It's only smart."

I didn't argue.

"So, you went to Shady Valley, correct?" I kept my thoughts on track.

"I did." He shifted nervously again. "I even went into the restaurant where we were supposed to meet. Then I saw her . . ."

"And?" Evie pressed, her voice rising with emotion.

A wistful smile washed over his features. "And she was beautiful. Gorgeous." His shoulders deflated. "And

I knew she'd never like me. She'd be so disappointed when she saw what I'm really like. I chickened out."

"You left?" Sherman asked.

"I did. I left before I could feel humiliated."

"My mom wasn't superficial," Evie said, still looking put off by the conversation and like she wanted to jam her heel into him.

"The issue is probably more with me than with women. I've dealt with it for my entire life."

Bob said he was nearly fifty, but he reminded me of an insecure, prepubescent high schooler—and slightly of Bob from *Stranger Things*.

"So you left? Without a word?" Evie continued. His story didn't seem to soften her up.

He shrugged again. "I did. I mean, for a minute."

"What's that mean?" Evie's voice rose higher.

"I mean, I chickened out. Walked away. And then I started to second-guess myself. I figured I shouldn't be such a wimp. I had my mind all made up. I went back into the restaurant, and I was going to be the man I'd always wanted to be."

"I sense there's a 'but' in there." Sherman pushed his glasses up higher, the analytical side of him shining through.

Good. We needed to use our strengths right now to find answers.

"That's correct." Bob glanced around. "When I went back inside, Angela was gone. I thought so, at least.

When I looked in the corner, I saw she was talking to this girl."

"Describe this girl," I said.

"I don't know. She was probably in her early twenties. She looked like she'd been crying. Angela was trying to comfort her."

"My mom has always had a soft spot for hurting people." Evie's voice cracked, and she rubbed her throat. "She was a foster kid herself. That's why she became a foster mom. Said it was important."

My heart pounded in my ears. Evie had just shared something personal. It wasn't something she often did, and I was honored that she'd opened up.

But right now, I needed to stay focused.

"What did you do next?" I turned my gaze back to Bob again.

He shrugged, his face flushing with embarrassment. "I left. I lost all my courage. I drove away, took down my profile, and resigned myself to being single for the rest of my life."

"Why did you run when you saw us?" That still didn't make sense. The reaction didn't match his story.

"I looked out the window and saw three strangers on my porch. I figured I was in trouble for something."

"Normal people just don't assume they're in trouble." Sherman crossed his arms and raised his brows, making it clear he didn't buy Bob's excuse.

"I do. I'm a hermit. People don't come visit me. I

don't know what to say. But that's the truth. Besides, I wondered if you were from that creepy little town."

My spine stiffened. "Shady Valley?"

"That's the one."

"If it's so creepy, why did you ask Angela to meet there?" What sense did that make?

"It wasn't my idea to meet there. It was Angela's."

I let the words settle in my mind. Why would Angela want to meet there? What about the town had drawn her?

My gut told me this guy was being honest. And, if he was, what had Angela Vance gotten herself involved with?

# CHAPTER
# TWELVE

AFTER LEAVING BOB'S, we got back in the car—Sherman in the front seat beside Evie, me in the back—and we sat there silently for a few minutes.

Finally, I asked, "So, what do you all think?"

"I believe him," Sherman said after another moment of thought. "I don't want to. I want to believe he has some answers that will lead us to Angela."

Evie crossed her arms. "He had all the signals to prove he's telling the truth. But I still don't like him. A grown man shouldn't be scared of women."

Sherman shrugged. "Women can be intimidating."

"No doubt. But women respect men who have courage enough to express their feelings. To take the bull by the horns. We want manly men."

I glanced at Sherman and saw his cheeks redden. I knew exactly what he was thinking. He'd been afraid of telling Evie how he felt—not unlike Bob. Evie's words were like a smack in the face. Compassion pounded inside me.

I decided to change the subject before Sherman could be further emasculated. "So, who was this woman Angela was talking to?"

"Your guess is as good as ours," Evie said.

I sat back and thought about it a moment, imagining the scenario playing out in my mind. Had Angela seen someone who was hurt or in trouble? Had she reached out—because that was just what Angela did?

I sat up straight, another thought hitting me.

"You know what? I have one more question. Excuse me a minute." I rushed from the car and pounded on Bob's door again.

He answered a moment later, looking confused and maybe even a little scared. "Yes?"

"Was there anything distinguishing about the young woman you saw talking with Angela?"

He thought about it a moment and shrugged. "She was wearing a gold necklace with a rose on it and another necklace with a skull. You mean stuff like that?"

"I mean, stuff exactly like that."

I remembered the unidentified body that had been found.

Only one fact stood out in my mind: the only thing personal found on that dead woman had been a rose necklace. What had happened to the other one?

"So Angela was talking to the woman who was later found dead?" Evie repeated as we headed down the road. "What does that mean?"

"We need to figure that out." I stared out the front window as my thoughts turned over. This new information left an uneasy feeling in my stomach.

"She wouldn't have done anything to that woman." Defensiveness edged into Evie's voice.

"No one said she would." I tried to tamp down the situation before our emotions became elevated. "I'm just afraid Angela got pulled into something she shouldn't have."

The words made my throat ache. But they were true. I knew we were all thinking the same thing, so there was no need to remain quiet, especially considering we were on borrowed time.

"You think Angela . . . might be dead also?" Evie's voice cracked, and she rubbed her neck.

"I didn't say that. I just don't like these connections we've discovered." Like, I really didn't like them. Not at all. Not even a smidgen of liking.

"Maybe the waitress at Pumpernickels will have more information for us." Sherman's voice sounded hopeful.

"Maybe," I said.

The rest of the ride was quiet. I knew I was lost in my own thoughts. Lost running through the what ifs.

I'd been certain that Angela's disappearance was connected with her online date. But it looked like I was wrong. Her disappearance may be connected with something much more sinister.

It wasn't the lead I'd been hoping for. Not in the least.

# CHAPTER
# THIRTEEN

THE THREE OF us agreed to go for a less assertive approach to talking to the waitress. Like Bob, she might go on the defensive if she saw three of us coming at her. But if we were seated at one of her tables . . . I figured that was our best bet to strike up conversation.

We stepped inside, and the heat warmed us. The day had grown chilly outside, and there'd even been talk of a few snow flurries tonight. It wasn't the springlike weather that I wanted.

Some soup sounded good. Maybe some coffee. But mostly I wanted answers. I craved them like a Neanderthal craved a big slab of woolly mammoth.

My gaze scanned the restaurant. It was just after lunchtime, and the place wasn't busy. The few people who were inside gave us their customary strange looks.

I spotted the waitress. She was working in the same

section of the dining area as she'd been last night. When the hostess asked to seat us, I pointed to her area.

"Could we be back there?" I asked. "By the windows?"

The stern, matronly woman looked in that direction and shrugged. "Sure."

A moment later, we were seated, and our waitress appeared.

The woman was probably in her mid-twenties. She had dark hair to her shoulders, all one length, and blue eyes. There was a certain kindness about her—but also a nervousness. I'd seen the hostess whisper something to the woman before she came over, and then they'd both glanced at us.

Did it go back to us being outsiders? Or was there more going on here?

"Hi, there." The waitress—Hillary was embroidered onto her green uniform—held her pad and pen in hand. "Can I get you something to drink?"

We all ordered water. When she came back a few minutes later and placed the drinks on the table, I decided to be a bit more chatty.

"What do you recommend?" I asked, holding a laminated menu.

"Oh, everything is good. It really is." She nodded, as if trying to convince herself.

"Any favorites?"

"The Reuben is always a hit."

"Then a Reuben it is." I closed my menu. "How long have you worked here? Seems like a pretty great place."

"Oh, it is. I've worked here since I was old enough to hold a tray."

"So you grew up here in Shady Valley?" I continued.

"I did. Never left. There are times I want to see the world." A wistful look crossed her eyes. "But my family is depending on me to help them out, so here I am."

I glanced back at the hostess, who watched us carefully. "I see. Your parents own this place?"

"They do." She swallowed hard and glanced back at the woman in the front. It had to be her mom. The woman's stern gaze could make anyone feel like they were being sent to time out. "Now, what can I get the rest of you?"

I wasn't finished with this discussion yet. But, for now, I would wait.

---

"I feel like we should be more aggressive," Evie nearly hissed from the other side of the table.

"Aggressive isn't always the right choice," I told her. "Just trust me."

Evie and Sherman were both great at working behind the scenes. Evie could put together an awesome profile, and Sherman was a computer guru. But I was the one most experienced when it came to the people side of the investigation equation. Sometimes, that seemed hard to believe, but I'd come a long way since I'd started doing this.

As a side note, "Investigation Equation" sounded like it could be a new song for *Schoolhouse Rock,* didn't it? I'd have to work on that later . . . maybe when I was out of work.

"I need to know what she knows." Evie's intense gaze bore into mine then Sherman's.

"And we will. Just be patient." Caution rose in me as I feared Evie might take matters into her own hands. I had to manage the waitress *and* Evie right now. One wrong move could ruin this.

Sherman's gaze swung back and forth between the two of us, as if he was on edge about the whole situation also.

A few minutes later, our food was delivered. Hillary caught my eye and offered a quick smile. I glanced behind her and saw that her mom—or the hostess, whom I *assumed* was her mom—was nowhere in sight. Maybe this was my opportunity.

"Hey, listen," I started, fearful that Evie would jump in if I didn't. "We've been looking for this woman. Have you seen her?"

Hillary looked behind her, swallowed hard, and then glanced at my phone quickly. "No, I don't think so."

"Are you sure? Could you look again?"

Her breaths came faster as her gaze skimmed my phone. "No, I haven't seen her. I'm sorry."

"Hillary, I have you on video talking to her." I lowered my voice. "I have a witness that places this woman in the restaurant."

She dropped her tray, and it clattered to the floor. She scrambled to pick it up, her hands shaking. "I wish I could help. I'm sorry."

And then she scurried away.

Evie's gaze met mine. "Why is she hiding something?"

"She looks scared," Sherman said.

I glanced through the kitchen doorway where she'd disappeared. "I agree. Something has her spooked. I have a feeling her parents are urging her silence."

The bigger question was why.

My gut twisted tighter as my uneasiness grew.

---

After we ate and paid the bill—Hillary's mom had brought us our checks, along with a dirty look—we stepped outside.

The rental car had been parked in front of the restaurant, and as I stared at it now, I realized something looked off.

That was when I realized the tires had all been slashed.

"You've got to be kidding me," I muttered. "Didn't this happen on our first case together also?"

"It did. Maybe we should get a license plate that reads 'Slashme.'"

Sherman had just made a joke. Kudos to him. Too bad I didn't feel like laughing right now.

He knelt down beside the car to examine the tires better. "These are all going to have to be replaced."

I wanted to kick something. Maybe a tire. But that wouldn't get me anywhere. Without a car, we were stuck here. The bed-and-breakfast was at least five miles away.

"Certainly, there's a mechanic somewhere in town," Evie said.

"I think we passed a shop earlier," I said. "But first we need to file a police report."

Evie snorted. "You really think those buffoons are going to do anything?"

I shrugged. "Not really. But you might need something official to present to the rental car company."

Chief Cruiser showed up five minutes after we called. He didn't seem to be in a hurry—not in the least. In fact, he stopped and talked to two different people on the sidewalk from the time he parked his car until he reached us. My irritation grew with every minute.

"So what do we have here?" He stared at our car, looking like he had all the time in the world and absolutely zero concern. As if to cement that fact, he reached into his pocket and pulled out a bag.

I watched as he pinched off something inside and stuck it in his cheek.

Tobacco? Really?

"Someone did this to our tires." I decided to explain it to him, just in case he didn't pick up on those facts by himself.

He examined the car, not getting too close. "That's interesting. Why would someone want to do this to you all?"

"You're the police chief. Maybe you can figure it out." My words had been snappy, and I hadn't intended that. But this man was just so maddening. Gone was my earlier helpless female persona. Now I was I'm-not-playing-no-games Gabby.

"I'll take your statements." He glared at me with a touch of rebellion in his gaze. "I don't expect to figure out who did this, though."

That was a resounding vote of confidence for his own crime-fighting abilities. I rolled my eyes.

"You could talk to people who may have been witnesses," Sherman said.

Cruiser nodded slowly, hooking his hands on his belt like he was some kind of washed-up eighties TV detective. "Yep, I guess I could do that."

"Or you could check security cameras around town," Sherman continued.

"We don't have none of those around here."

"Sure you do. You have at least five."

Cruiser raised his eyebrows. "How would you know that?"

Sherman shrugged, his cheeks reddening slightly. "What can I say? I'm observant."

This man had no intention of looking further into this. What was his problem?

"I'm sorry, are we interrupting a game you're watching on TV?" I asked. "Because this is a crime, and I don't think you're taking it seriously."

He silently assessed me with his gaze. "Oh, I assure you. I'm taking it seriously. We always take it seriously when trouble comes into town."

For some reason, I thought he was talking about us and not the vandalism of our vehicle. Was that how this guy perceived visitors?

It was people like him who gave cops a bad name.

I couldn't let this go, but I also knew I couldn't fight through simply confronting this man. I wouldn't get far. But there was more than one way to handle a situation like this.

Instead, I nodded coolly. "I'll be following up on your report then."

Someone was clearly sending us a message. We weren't welcome here.

But why?

# CHAPTER
# FOURTEEN

WHILE SHERMAN and Evie went into the garage to take care of the tires, I remained outside and pulled out my phone.

One of the good things about working for Grayson Tech was that I'd made contacts with local law enforcement departments. I'd gone in, done my workshop, hung out with the troopers there, and exchanged contact information in case they had questions after I left.

I'd developed solid relationships with some of them. A couple people I'd worked with had even offered me a job if I ever left Grayson Tech. I might have to revisit some of those offers when this was over.

Only a month or so ago, I'd done a presentation with a Pennsylvania State Police office in Harrisburg. One of the detectives, Lt. Daniel Yoder, had been especially personable.

I gave him a call, and he answered on the first ring.

"If it's not Gabby Thomas," he said. "How can I help you?"

"It's good to hear your voice, Daniel." I shivered as a chilly breeze swept down the street. Trying to ward off the cold, I stepped behind the building, hoping it would block the wind. It did—a little, at least.

"Tell that to the punk I just arrested for vandalizing three businesses in the area."

I smiled and imagined the burly detective explaining the cold, hard facts of life to the vandals. "Listen, Daniel, I'm here in Shady Valley, PA."

He made a clucking sound with his tongue.

"What's that mean?" I glanced around the town, but I didn't see anyone else nearby to overhear my conversation. I would need to be careful if I wanted to make any progress with this case.

"That place is backward."

He had that right. "You've been here before?"

"No, I don't have to go there. The rumor mill has told me enough. When that town started to die, only a few families remained. Now they run everything, and think they're above the law."

That sounded about right. I leaned against the wall, and the rough bricks behind me snagged my hair. "I can't argue with that. But I do have a question for you."

"Shoot," Daniel said.

"I came here because my friend's mom disappeared. In the course of my investigation, we've discovered there was an unidentified female found dead here just over a month ago. Strangled. I can hardly find any media coverage for it, and the local police don't seem very interested."

"Tell me more."

I paused as someone revved their engine close by. A motorcycle rounded the corner, the same man I'd seen before riding it. I waited until he passed before I said, "Honestly, I don't think the police have done anything to try and figure out who this woman is or what happened to her. It's disturbing."

"Are you talking about the dead woman or your missing friend?"

"Honestly? Either. I was wondering if you'd heard anything or if this is a special situation where you could send in someone else to oversee this place. Their lack of professionalism is an injustice."

"Let me look into this more. I won't give you an answer now. I mean, we don't know for a fact that nothing has been done, and officials aren't obligated to share a play-by-play of their investigations with you. At this point, you're assuming they've done nothing but have no proof of it."

"I suppose that's true." Assumptions were going to be the death of me. But my assumptions were so often right . . . until they weren't. And then they nearly got me killed.

"I'm going to make some calls. I'll give you a call back later."

"Sounds great. Thank you."

"Hang tight. And be careful. It sounds like you could be stirring up trouble. Towns like Shady Valley . . . they're not going to be welcoming of that."

My throat tightened. "So I've gathered."

As I paced through the alley, I paused and observed the parking lot behind the buildings.

A truck was parked there.

I recognized it. It was the same one that had driven past Helene's yesterday and tried to light her place on fire.

It would take two hours to change the tires out. That meant we had two hours to kill in downtown Shady Valley. It wasn't exactly what I wanted to do considering what a tight schedule we were on. But our only other option was to call Helene and see if she could pick us up. We might have to do that, if worse came to worst.

But for now, I wanted to pay a visit to Cruiser's General Store. It was located in one of the old buildings lining Main Street, and it seemed like a good place to pass time and get out of the cold. Plus, that's where the truck had been parked.

As soon as we walked in, the woman behind the counter scowled at us. She was in her forties with messy light-brown hair and a haggard gaze. Her eyes were on us from the moment we stepped inside.

"I feel so uncomfortable right now," Evie muttered as we began browsing the outer wall where some garden flags were hanging.

"Me too." Sherman leaned closer and barely moved his lips. "Why is she watching us? Does she think we're going to steal something?"

"It's because we don't belong here," I said. "The Cruiser family owns this place. They run this whole town."

"Can I help you?" a deep voice bellowed.

I sucked in a quick breath when I saw the large, meaty man standing at the end of the aisle. Not only was he large, but he had a beard that could win an award from the National Hipster Association of Nonhipsters and a deep voice that rivaled James Earl Jones—only menacing.

Was this the man who'd thrown the Molotov cocktail?

"We're just looking around," I said. I picked up a cheerful flag that read "BEE Kind" and waved it as a subliminal reminder.

"I know who you are." He narrowed his gaze.

My lungs tightened as my internal alarms told me he could be dangerous. "Do you?"

"I've seen you wandering around town, asking questions."

I pulled out Angela's picture, deciding to use this opportunity to my advantage. "You ever seen this woman?"

He didn't even look at her photo. "No, I can't say I have."

"Can you look closer?"

"Don't need to," he growled.

He put his hands on his hips, making himself look even larger than he actually was. The action was unnecessary considering how big he already looked. "Now, unless you're going to buy something, I'm going to have to ask you to leave."

Any sane person would have left. Me? I strode toward the counter and grabbed a candy bar. "I'll take one of these then."

He grunted.

Slowly, I slapped the chocolate treat on the wooden surface there. The woman barely looked at me as she rang up the bar. My gaze latched on her neck.

The necklace there . . . it had a skull on it.

Just like the one Bob had mentioned seeing on the woman Angela was speaking with. The woman who'd ended up dead.

"That will be $1.28," the cashier said.

I pulled my gaze away. I wanted to say something. More than anything I did. But I knew that man behind me was just looking for a reason to get physical. I couldn't give him one.

Instead, I pulled the money from my wallet and left it on the counter. "Keep the change."

I nodded to my friends, and we walked toward the exit. So much for killing time in here.

"What are these people's problems?" Evie asked as soon as we were outside.

"That's a great question," Sherman said. "They definitely don't like us."

"Guys, that woman was wearing a skull necklace," I turned toward them, my heart racing.

Neither said anything for a moment, but I knew what they were thinking. We had a lead. That cashier might know something about the woman who'd been found dead here in town.

"What do we do now?" Sherman said.

"I'll let Daniel know." It was a good starting point, at least.

Just then, Evie's phone rang. She mumbled a few things before turning to me.

"The garage doesn't have four tires like they said they did," Evie said. "It's not going to be ready until tomorrow."

My eyes narrowed.

Strange that he hadn't checked before we left. It also

made me wonder if he was telling the truth or if someone had persuaded him to change his story. Either way, I knew Evie and Sherman weren't getting their rental back today.

I turned to my friends. It looked like we were going to have to call Helene for a ride after all.

# CHAPTER
# FIFTEEN

TWENTY MINUTES LATER, we'd all climbed into George's pickup truck and we bounced down the road. The scent of horses and dried grass permeated the inside of the truck and reminded me about what was at stake.

This was about more than Angela. It was about people who'd been wronged by others—people who had lives and livelihoods that were being threatened.

My thoughts went back to that necklace I'd seen on that woman. I needed to tell someone about it—but it wouldn't be Chief Cruiser.

"Someone slashed your tires, huh?" George stared out the windshield and shook his head.

I crossed my arms, liking this town less and less all the time. "That's right."

"Who did you tick off?"

"I didn't think we'd ticked anyone off yet," I said. "We're just starting to turn over stones. What's up with this town?"

"If you haven't noticed, the Cruisers pretty much run things. If something doesn't go their way, they do something about it. They consider this their turf."

"How long have you lived here?" Evie asked, poking her head forward from the backseat. "Are you an outsider too?"

"I've been here about two-and-a-half years. Lived in upstate New York before this. But when family needs you, you do what you can to help."

"That was nice of you," I said.

He shrugged like it wasn't a big deal. "I'm retired and just work for fun and for some extra spending money."

"What do you do?" Evie asked. "Besides help with the farm."

"I work a part-time job with the state—enough to pay my bills—and to try to help Helene."

"I'm sorry to hear about your brother," I told him.

He frowned. "Me too. It was a tragedy. He loved riding horses more than anything. It was his dream to buy this place. To work the land. Have some animals."

"I'm glad Helene was able to stay."

"It hasn't been easy on her. She pretty much left everyone behind to have this life with Tom. When he died . . . she was alone. The two weren't able to have kids, so it was just them. They were happy that way, though."

"It's nice she's been able to keep the farm going."

"The bed-and-breakfast helps pay for some expenses. The Cruisers would like her gone, of course. Like I said, they don't like outsiders, and her place brings in outsiders."

"Do you think they're the ones who let the horses out last night?" I asked, still trying to form a complete picture.

George shrugged. "I wouldn't put it past them. I keep telling Helene to move. To sell the place. Maybe she could make some money and start fresh."

"But she doesn't want to?" I asked.

"No, this is her home, and she doesn't want to be run off. I can't really blame her—I only want her to be happy. That's what Tom would have wanted."

My thoughts continued churning, finally stopping when I remembered a conversation I'd had with George when we'd first met. "Tell me about Laurie."

She was another missing woman. Was she from this area? Did she somehow fit in with all of this? I mentally kicked myself for not considering it sooner.

"Laurie?" He let out a breath and squeezed his steering wheel harder. "I don't know what to say. She was the love of my life."

"When did you say she disappeared?" I asked.

"About two years ago."

Two years ago? That didn't really fit our profile. But I still wanted to hear more. "What happened?"

"She went out one night to go to the store. She never returned. No one heard from her. No one found her car. Nothing."

A chill swept over my spine. "Where were you living at the time?"

"Here in Shady Valley. She wasn't from here. She lived in a town about an hour north."

"I'm sorry, George," I said. "I guess the police didn't have any leads."

"None. It was almost like she disappeared off the face of the earth."

We pulled up to the bed-and-breakfast.

This wasn't over. We were still going to find answers. About Jane Doe. About Angela. Maybe even about Laurie.

And I knew exactly what I wanted to do next.

***

While Sherman and Evie researched why Angela might have chosen Shady Valley, I hopped into my car and headed back into town.

If someone thought slashed tires were going to slow me down, they were so, so wrong.

I parked in the lot behind the buildings on Main

Street and glanced around. I saw no one. I hoped that also meant that no one was watching me.

I'd found a space near Pumpernickels, and from this vantage point I could see everyone coming and going from the back door of the restaurant. I planned to stay until I saw Hillary leave.

She knew something. I was certain of it. I wanted to know what she knew.

She'd never speak to me in front of her family.

That meant I needed to catch her alone.

I was too restless to remain in my car, so I walked to the sidewalk and paused near the corner. From here, I could view both the alley and the parking lot.

Even though it was obvious that I wasn't welcome in this town, I wasn't one to shrink away from trouble. Did the fact that I wasn't welcome mean that I was in danger? I couldn't answer that yet. But discomfort jostled inside me.

I looked at my watch. It was almost five o'clock. I wondered how long Hillary would work before she would need to take a break. Certainly there were laws about these things. But since she worked for her family, all those rules might be out the window. That wasn't going to stop me from trying.

I pulled my coat closer as a chilly wind swept down the street, bringing with it a few unseasonable, stray snow flurries. I was so ready for some warmer weather.

I saw a chip bag on the ground and reached down to

swoop it up. One of the self-help books I'd been reading had encouraged me to do small acts that would leave the world a better place. I shoved the wrapper into my pocket until I could find a trash can.

One act for the day was done.

As I waited, my mind drifted to my job situation again. I had to tell Riley. But my news would affect him and his future, and that thought made regret squeeze my heart. More than anything, I wanted him to be happy. I wanted him to be able to reach for the stars and achieve his dreams. The last thing I wanted was to hold him back, and that's exactly what I felt might happen.

When I dropped out of college while studying forensics, I had needed something to do to make money. I'd turned to crime-scene cleaning because it helped keep me connected with police investigations in a vague, unofficial way. I had managed to find evidence that the police had missed on more than one occasion. I had made friends, and I'd made enemies.

It hadn't been a bad job. In fact, I was pretty fond of those early days in my career. Without them, I may not have met Riley or Sierra or Chad or so many of the friends that I had now. In fact, it was my start. Those choices had eventually led me to get the job with Grayson Tech.

I let out a sigh. So much weighed heavily on my mind.

I stared at the restaurant again. Still no movement. But a noise on the street made me turn my ear.

I recognized that sound.

A motorcycle.

Just then, the driver pulled into the lot and parked in a space. When he pulled his helmet off, his gaze was on me.

# CHAPTER
## SIXTEEN

I WATCHED as the man climbed off his Harley, left his helmet on the back, and strode toward me. I braced myself for whatever might happen next.

Would he walk past? Should I talk to him? Run for my life?

As much as he seemed to drive around this area, maybe he knew something. But even if he did, would he tell me?

He nodded at me, his blue eyes icy cold. He continued past me but, before he reached the sidewalk, he paused.

"New in town?" His voice sounded low but surprisingly cultured. The man was probably in his mid-fifties with silver hair and surprisingly smooth skin. He didn't scream motorcycle gang member, more like someone with money who'd gone through a mid-life crisis.

"Just visiting," I told him.

"I've seen you around. We don't get many visitors here."

"I had that impression." My muscles tensed as I waited to see where this conversation would go. "You seem to like riding around town a lot."

He crossed his arms. "I like to keep an eye on things."

Was he one of those locals who liked to "protect" the area? That was my impression.

"I see." On a whim, I pulled out my phone and pulled up Angela's picture. "You ever seen this woman?"

He glanced at the phone before nodding. "I did. I talked to her."

"What did she say?"

"She asked me if I'd seen a girl."

"What girl?"

His gaze darkened. "The same one who turned up dead in our municipal park."

My breath caught. "What did you tell her?"

"I told her I'd seen the girl around."

"Did she say how she knew her? Anything else?" This was my chance at finding answers. I prayed he would share whatever he knew.

"No, but she looked frantic," the man said. "That's all I know. Now, if there's nothing else, I'll be going . . ."

Before I could say anything else, he strode away. But I had a feeling he had more answers. I just had to figure out how to get him to share.

---

I continued leaning against the corner for a while until, finally, I moved back into my car. I could see the door to Pumpernickels from in there, and it was warmer.

My mind lingered on my conversation with Motorcycle Man. What did he know? And how was I going to get him to tell me?

I wasn't sure.

Before I could figure it out, my phone rang. I saw Garrett Mercer's number and answered.

"Hey, you," I said. Garrett was the man who funded this humble little operation.

He was like Townsend, and the rest of us were like Charlie's Angels—only Sherman wasn't a female, and Evie would call the name sexist. Oh, and Garrett was actually a coffee mogul instead of the head of a private investigation agency. Still, I thought the comparison had merit.

He'd started our squad because his own family had been murdered. I'd helped him find the killer and, in the process, find some closure. He funded this operation as his way of giving back.

"Gabby, I just wanted to check in." His British voice rolled across the line. "How are things?"

I gave him a nutshell update.

"Things are always exciting with you, aren't they?" he said, a tease to his voice.

"Yes, they are." No one could argue that point.

His voice turned serious. "Listen, I heard about Grayson Tech. Margo called me. Sorry for the bad news."

"Thanks for the sympathy. It was a surprise, to say the least."

"If there's anything I can do, let me know. And I hope you find your girl up there in Pennsylvania. If anyone can do it, it's you guys. I'd put my money on it."

"Nice one."

He chuckled. "I thought so too."

I appreciated his faith in us because I didn't always share the sentiment. Sometimes I felt like I had no idea what I was doing.

I ended the call and stared at the backside of Pumpernickels again.

I was nearly ready to call it a night. I couldn't stay out here but for so long. There were other things I needed to do, and if Hillary left this location with somebody else, my time would be wasted because I still would not be able to speak with her.

Just as the thought entered my mind, the back door

to the restaurant opened. I straightened and held my breath as I watched.

Maybe my luck was turning around. Hillary stepped out, a bag of trash in her hands. I knew if I wanted to talk to her, it was now or never.

# CHAPTER SEVENTEEN

I RUSHED TOWARD HILLARY, not wanting to scare her but not wanting to miss this opportunity either.

"Hillary!" I called.

She looked up, a flash of alarm in her eyes. She looked to the left and the right, as if either contemplating running or looking to see if anybody else was around. Quickly, she threw the bag into a dumpster and then took a step back toward the door.

"I can't talk," she called over her shoulder.

I stopped near the steps and tried to catch my breath. I'd run faster than I'd realized. "Please. I just need a minute of your time."

"I have nothing to say to you." She reached for the door handle.

"What are you afraid of?"

She froze and jerked her gaze toward me. "I'm not afraid of nothing."

"Then why won't you answer my question?"

She shrugged so quickly it almost looked like a flinch. "Because there's more at stake here than meets the eye."

I stepped closer and softened my voice. "All I want to do is find a woman who is missing. Her name is Angela Vance, and her daughter is worried sick about her. Why is it too much to ask if you have seen anything?"

Hillary looked around again before crossing her arms. She moved closer and lowered her voice. "Yes, I did see that woman in this restaurant a month or two ago."

My heart raced. "What do you remember about her?"

She swallowed hard, obviously uncomfortable. "I recognize most of the people who come in here from out of town. We don't get a lot of visitors. And we rarely ever have any returning visitors. I saw that woman come in, and she asked for a booth in the corner. She sat facing the door, and she watched it like she was waiting for somebody. But nobody ever came."

I waited for her to continue. Her gaze shifted, as if she was still nervous. I feared she'd change her mind, but she didn't.

"A man also came in. He looked at this woman—

Angela, right?—and then he turned around and left. I was curious, but I didn't ask any questions. The woman didn't see him."

My pulse pounded in my ears, and I prayed this conversation wouldn't be interrupted. "What happened then?"

"A few minutes later somebody else came in. It was like Grand Central Station that evening. It was a girl. Maybe I shouldn't say girl. She was probably my age, but she seemed younger, you know?"

"I know the type."

"Anyway, this girl seemed desolate or something. Looked like she had been crying and hadn't taken a shower for a while. I wondered if she was homeless."

I stored away those new facts. "Did she ask for a seat?"

"She did, and I almost didn't seat her. Mama don't like riffraff in here. She doesn't like trouble. But I seated her anyway. She was at a table by herself and, when she looked at the menu, she nearly started crying. I figured she didn't have money. Next thing I knew that woman you were talking about, that Angela lady . . . she went over and sat beside her. She ordered food for her and paid with cash. Then she sat beside her, and they talked and talked and talked."

From what Evie had said about Angela, that fit her MO. She loved helping hurt people. "Did anything else happen?"

"That man came back in. He looked over and saw Angela with that woman, and he left again. Strange one, he was. He seemed nervous, you know? But Angela never saw him—not to my knowledge, at least."

"Did Angela leave with the girl?"

Hillary scanned the parking lot again. "No, a few minutes later, the girl left. Angela sat in the booth by herself for several minutes. Finally, she got up also and asked if she could talk to me for a minute."

This must be the moment that was caught on the video camera on the sidewalk. I held my breath, anticipating what Hillary would say next.

"I stepped outside. Took a five-minute break. I was hoping Angela might tell me what's going on. Not a lot of exciting things happen here in this town, and I felt like there was a story behind all of this."

"What did she say?" Was this the turning point I'd been waiting for in this investigation?

"She asked if there were any shelters around here or somewhere where that woman might be able to get some help. Said the gal didn't have anywhere to go and was running from a bad situation."

"And you told her?"

"I told her there wasn't anything around here, that maybe she should try one of the bigger cities. They had more to offer."

"What did she say?" We were finally getting somewhere. Excitement zinged through my blood.

"She said she was going to go after that girl, that someone needed to help her."

"Did you realize the girl was the same person who ended up dead in the park two days later?"

Hillary's face fell, and she looked down at the ground. "Yes, I knew that. I felt terrible about it, but I didn't know what else I should've done. I don't know how else I should've helped. Besides, I thought that Angela woman was helping her. I never saw either of them again."

"Did you tell the police chief about it?"

Hillary looked back up at me, but something changed in her gaze. She shifted, as if uncomfortable. "Yeah, I told him."

"And what did he say?" Did he receive the news better because it came from a local?

"He took the information, but he didn't seem all that interested. He said he'd keep his eyes open."

"Did you find that weird? Why is he so aloof?" I wanted her insight into the man.

Hillary shrugged and frowned. "That's just the way he is."

I wanted more than that. "Why doesn't that bother you?"

Her gaze met mine, a deep emotion hovering there. "I reckon it don't. After all, he's been my boyfriend for the past three years."

I got back to the bed-and-breakfast that evening, still processing everything that Hillary had told me. I didn't know what to think or why the police chief wasn't doing his job. But I didn't intend to leave this town without doing something about it.

One cop should not paint all cops in a bad light. What was that saying? One bad apple can ruin the bunch. This investigation seemed to be a case in point.

As soon as I got back upstairs, Sherman and Evie met me, and I gave them the update. We all sat in Evie's room, which was the largest. It even had a little settee and table near the double doors leading to a second-story balcony.

"What do you think all this means?" Sherman shoved his hands into the kangaroo pocket of his Yale sweatshirt as he waited for our response.

"I have no idea," I said. "But, Evie, it's like you have said all this time—Angela really did have a heart to help other people. I just hope that didn't get her in trouble."

Evie rubbed the bottom of her eye. I wondered if there may have been a tear there. She would never admit it, though, would she? But she seemed especially somber since I'd given her the update.

"If she went with that woman who ended up dead, who's to say she didn't end up that way as well?" Evie's voice cracked.

Sherman laid a hand on her back, and, to my surprise, Evie didn't flinch or pull away. "If she wasn't alive, most likely her body would've also turned up by now," he murmured.

"I know that." Evie let out a long breath, and I could tell she was trying to remain in control. "Profiling is what I do. And you're right. That should make me feel better, but somehow it doesn't. Angela got wrapped up in all of this, and I have no idea what might've happened to her as a result."

"We are slowly but surely getting some answers here," Sherman said. "We just need to keep pushing."

Evie nodded slowly. "You're right. We need to stick with the facts right now. So Angela went to catch up with this woman who ended up dead. The question is, did Angela ever end up catching her or not? What exactly happened next?"

"I'm not sure if we will ever know that. Not until we find Angela and we can ask her."

"We need to figure out what happened in the time in between," Sherman said. "Two days passed, correct?"

"That's correct," I said. "We need to add this to our timeline. And, by the way, Hillary corroborated what Robert Murphy told us. His story matches."

"So maybe we really can clear him." Sherman pushed his glasses up on his nose again.

He really needed to have those tightened sometime.

"At least, preliminarily." Evie frowned as if disappointed.

I stared at my friend for a moment. What was buried deep inside that head of hers? What was she really thinking? I had no idea.

I shifted. "If you had to put together a profile of this killer, Evie, what would it look like?"

She was silent for a moment. "I really don't have enough to go on, especially not without seeing an official police report or autopsy. But the fact that this woman's body was left in a park instead of hidden away makes me think that this killer wanted to be known."

I shivered. This killer wanted to be known.

That indicated an entirely different kind of evil. That could mean this wasn't a crime that had happened in the heat of the moment. It wasn't an accident.

Someone had wanted to send a message.

Before we could go any further, I heard a noise outside the window. I opened the balcony door and pulled my sweater closer before I stepped outside.

My eyes widened with alarm when I saw a group of men standing on the lawn.

I had a feeling they weren't here selling Amway.

# CHAPTER
# EIGHTEEN

EVIE AND SHERMAN stepped out behind me, and I heard their gasps.

"What in the world . . . ?" Sherman said.

I scanned the faces. There were six men. As if synchronized, flames ignited in their hands.

Torches? Who in the world carried torches anymore?

The fact that I even had to ask that question was bone-chilling. They'd brought those so they could send a message. They'd succeeded.

One of the men looked up at me. I recognized him. He was the burly man from Cruiser's General Store. Anger blazed in his eyes.

"You're not welcome here!" he yelled up at us. "We don't want you in this town."

"It's a free country," I called back. "We're not bothering you."

"All you're doing is stirring up trouble, and we don't like it."

"All we're trying to do is find answers." My hands gripped the railing, and I felt a tremble rake through me.

I'd been in a lot of bad situations before, but never one like this. If those men were to throw their torches, this whole place could go up in flames. Not only would our lives be on the line, but so would Helene's livelihood.

Based on the look in those men's eyes, I wouldn't put it past them to do just that. It wasn't that they didn't have a conscience. They were woefully misled and thought that they were doing the right thing. Maybe that was worse.

"Gabby," Evie whispered in my ear.

I heard the fear there. It wasn't an emotion I often heard from Ms. Stone-Cold and Unemotional. But something like this could shake up the strongest people.

I watched as a new figure emerged from around the corner. George. He had a shotgun in his hands.

"Get off my property!" He raised a gun to his shoulder.

"Last I heard this wasn't your property," the general store man called back. "It's your brother's."

"I oversee this property, and, I'm telling you, you need to leave."

"What are you going to do? Call the police chief?" The men begin cackling with laughter.

George cocked his gun. "I mean it. You need to leave. Now."

The General Store man glanced back up at us and glared. "You got our message. You have twenty-four hours. Next time we see you, we aren't going to be so friendly."

I held my breath, anxious to see if the men would really leave or not. Concerned about whether they would take their torches with them or if they would hurl them at the house instead. Uneasy, I wondered if George would become a victim while defending Helene's property. There was no good ending to the situation, was there?

Finally, their torches were snuffed out, and the men all jumped into the old pickup truck that I had seen drive past on my first day here. The one whose passenger had thrown out the Molotov cocktail.

A moment later, they squealed away.

I let out a long breath. My life had flashed before my eyes for a minute there. Things just kept getting worse and worse in this town. We had to figure out what we were going to do about it, and, apparently, we had even less time than we thought.

---

Evie, Sherman, and I rushed downstairs to check on Helene. We found her in the entryway. George had come inside, and he had his arms around her. She wept in his embrace.

An ache panged through me, and I stepped forward. "Helene, I am so sorry."

She stepped from George's arms and turned toward me. When her eyes met mine, I saw a moment of accusation there. She very well might want us to leave right now. I waited for confirmation.

"You can't let those men bully you around," she finally said, her voice hoarse with emotion.

I blinked, surprised at her words. "We wouldn't blame you if you wanted us to go."

"You can't let them win," she said.

"Helene . . ." George reached for her again but dropped his arm. "You have to think of yourself. Those men could ruin you."

"He's right," I said. "Those men weren't playing. If we're not gone in twenty-four hours, I have no doubt they're going to come back and they're going to carry through with the completion on their threat. I don't want to put you in the middle of this."

"I've always been in the middle of this. They hated my husband, Tom, and they've never let me forget it." Helene's face looked pinched with stress.

"Why did they hate Tom so much?" I asked, knowing there had to be more to this story.

Helene raised her chin, a far-off look in her eyes. "Big Frankie came here once, asking for donations to

Chief Cruiser's 'benevolence fund.' Everyone knows he doesn't have a real charity, that he pockets the money."

"Who's Big Frankie?" Sherman asked.

"He runs the General Store. He's also Chief Cruiser's uncle."

So that was his name. I stored the information away.

"Anyway, Tom refused to help," Helene said. "Big Frankie told him he should think about it some more. They came back the next night, and Tom refused again. They've made our lives miserable ever since."

Though it didn't surprise me, it just confirmed how despicable these men were.

"You could just sell this place." George's voice hardened with conviction. "You don't need it. And besides, it's a lot to take care of. Maybe you could get yourself a condo down in Lancaster, or even go down to Florida and get far away from this area."

"If there's one thing Tom taught me it was to stand my ground. There's no way I am going to let evil men get away with evil deeds just because I'm scared. It's not the way I want to live my life." Her voice trembled with determination.

I had to give Helene credit. I hadn't taken her for the courageous type. She seemed too meek and humble to stand up for herself like this. But I was proud of her for doing so. She was a true example of a strong but quiet woman.

"I'll respect whatever decision you make," I said. "Why don't you sleep on it?"

"My mind is made up." Her gaze locked with mine. "You are all staying for as long as you would like to stay. I have ways to defend myself."

"But if they come back with fire—" I started.

"Then if I perish, I perish."

Silence fell on me. I remembered the verse from the Bible, from the story of Esther. Queen Esther had been an incredibly brave woman who was willing to do the right thing no matter the cost. So was Helene.

Finally, after a moment, I took a step back and nodded. "I'll let you two talk then. We'll see you in the morning. If you need anything, you know where to find us."

Back upstairs, Sherman turned toward me. "Do you think we should leave?"

"I don't know," I said. "I admire her bravery, but I don't want to put her in harm's way."

Evie was surprisingly silent beside us.

I turned toward her. "What are you thinking?"

"I'm thinking that Helene just taught me a lesson."

I'd halfway expected something sarcastic, but she sounded surprisingly sincere. "What's that?"

"When I met Helene, I thought she was weak. In fact, I pitied her. But seeing her tonight reminded me that strong women don't always look the same."

She didn't offer any more, and she didn't need to.

That admission coming from Evie was enough within itself. Maybe some of the ice around Evie's heart was finally beginning to melt.

"Maybe you should get some rest." Sherman studied Evie, a crease of worry forming between his eyes.

Evie didn't argue. She nodded and walked to her doorway before pausing. She turned toward us, a new look of gratitude in her gaze. "I'll talk to you both in the morning. Thank you both for everything. You've put your lives on the line to help me. I don't know if anyone's ever done something that nice for me, and I know that I'm not always the most grateful and appreciative person. I apologize for that."

I blinked, stunned into silence. It was like the nice person I'd always known was buried deep down inside Evie was emerging after years of being dormant.

Just then Sherman's phone rang. He looked at the screen quickly before putting it away.

"Your girlfriend?" Evie asked.

"She's not actually my girlfriend," Sherman said. "We're just chatting."

Evie frowned. "Then you should go and call her back. Good night, everyone."

# CHAPTER
## NINETEEN

AS I GOT BACK to my room, I realized that my adrenaline was still pumping. Every time I closed my eyes, I saw those men outside the house. I smelled the smoke from their torches. I heard the venom in their voices.

I shivered as I leaned against my door a minute. There were no guarantees that they wouldn't come back tonight. Men like that weren't men of their word, always holding up their side of the bargain. They could very well be determined to teach us a lesson either way.

What exactly had we done that made them feel so threatened? Was it because I talked to Hillary earlier? Had they found out about it, and had that been the tipping point?

Who was the ringleader of the bunch? Police Chief Cruiser? Big Frankie? The man on the motorcycle?

Motorcycle Man still had me curious. He appeared to be watching us, and I couldn't figure out why. If I were honest, part of me was tempted to just flee this place. To get out while we could before we got in any deeper.

But running away wasn't in my DNA. I needed to find answers, and I had no time to waste.

Maybe, in a way, I was like Helene. I didn't like for people to bully me and tell me what to do. I never had and I never would. In fact, in some ways, having those men show up here tonight made me want to fight even harder.

I picked up my phone. I really did need to call Riley. With everything that had happened today, I hadn't had a chance to talk to him yet.

Besides, the announcement to all of the Grayson Tech employees was supposed to take place today. I didn't want Riley to find out from anyone other than me. I didn't think he had connections with anybody else at the company, but I shouldn't chance it.

Just then, my phone rang. I looked at the screen and saw it was my friend Lt. Daniel Yoder from Harrisburg. Maybe he had an update for me.

I answered, happy to delay the inevitable for a few more minutes. "Hey, Daniel. What's going on?"

"I am sorry to be calling so late," he started. "But there was something I thought you would want to know. I couldn't wait until the morning."

I straightened, more anxious than ever to hear what he had to share with me.

---

"What did you find out?" I pushed away from the door and began pacing.

"You are not going to believe this, Gabby. I'm glad you brought this case to my attention, because I discovered a few things I think you'll find very interesting."

"Do tell."

"I put the information into the database and started digging around a little bit. It turns out that there have been four different women in four different counties within an hour radius of Shady Valley who've turned up dead over the past two years."

I sucked in a breath, uncertain if I'd heard correctly. "Four dead women?"

"That's right. Each of the deaths is unsolved. Because the crimes took place in different counties, law officials failed to connect the dots that they might all be related. When I looked into the details of each case, there were some striking similarities."

He had my full attention. "Like what?"

"For starters, all of the women were in their early twenties and they all had sad stories."

"Keep going."

"Each of them was strangled and left for dead in a

public place. Any suspects eventually fizzled out, leaving them as cold cases. The thing is, with these girls, they didn't have families who pushed law enforcement officials to continue searching for answers. At least, that's how it appears. Each of these women were pretty much alone in the world. Now that we know about the similarities, the state police are going to step in and investigate."

Excitement raced through me. Take that, Chief Cruiser. No longer would he be able to sweep this under the rug. He was going to have to face the facts. I hoped that somehow, he would pay for all the mistakes he had already made. But that was all secondary to finding out what happened to these girls.

I sat on the edge of my bed. "Is there any way I can get information on these women?"

"I can send over what I know, but you can't show it to anybody."

"I have two colleagues here with me, and we're trying to find a woman who doesn't fit your profile. I promise we will use discretion."

"I know you will. I'll send that information now."

"Thanks. I appreciate that."

Before I ended the call, Daniel called my name. "Yes?"

"I heard about Grayson Tech, that they are having to get rid of half of their workforce. I am sorry to hear that. Did you make the cut?"

The information about what had happened had been leaked. That meant that Riley could have potentially heard. "No, I won't have a job in a month."

"I'm sorry to hear that. If there are job openings around here, I'd be happy to let you know."

"If you wouldn't mind, please do that."

I ended the call and knew I needed to call Riley. But first I had to tell Evie and Sherman what I had just learned.

# CHAPTER
## TWENTY

"DON'T YOU SEE?" I asked, staring at Evie and Sherman as we gathered again in Evie's room. "This is good news."

"How is it good news?" Evie blinked, some of her off-putting tendencies returning.

"Angela doesn't fit this description," I said. "She's not in her twenties, and she wasn't a loner without a family to look for her. Besides, like Daniel said, all the other women were found dead within a couple of days of going missing and their bodies left in a public place. If Angela was a victim, she would've appeared by now."

"This is all disturbing." Sherman crossed his arms, partially covering his Batman shirt. He also wore matching pajama bottoms. He obviously hadn't planned on seeing us again this evening.

"I know," I agreed. "In fact, the deeper we get into this, the more disturbed I am."

"The only conclusion I can think of is that Angela somehow tried to help this woman who was found in Shady Valley, and she got pulled into something dangerous." Evie tapped her foot and stared at the wall, her mind looking a million miles away. "Just because her body hasn't turned up, that doesn't mean good things for her."

I understood what she was saying, and I couldn't argue. The fact that Angela hadn't been seen for more than a month wasn't a good sign. But the fact that her body hadn't turned up still gave me hope.

"So what does this mean for us?" Sherman pushed up his glasses. "Where do we go from here?"

"I'm going to send you the file that Daniel just sent me—for your eyes alone. We can each review the victims. I suggest that we do this individually, and then we come together and share our conclusions. That way our opinions don't taint each other's. Sound good?"

"Sounds reasonable," Evie said. "If I can put together a profile, I will. I should have enough information to start since we will have a list of the victims."

I said good night to them for the second time. As I walked into my room, I glanced out the window. It looked peaceful outside, except for . . . movement in the corner of the yard. I sucked in a breath, waiting to see if more trouble had shown up.

Instead, George came into focus. He sat on his porch, his gun in hand, on the lookout for trouble.

The thought did bring me a little comfort. At least somebody was watching out for us.

With all of my boxes checked off, I had no other excuses not to call Riley. I stared at the phone for just a moment before dialing his number. He answered on the first ring.

"Hey, gorgeous. I was wondering if you were going to call today."

I smiled at his warm greeting and then filled him in on everything that was going on with the case.

"I don't like the sound of any of this, Gabby. I thought it was going to be a simple case, but I can see that it is not."

"We all feel the same way. This is turning into something much bigger than any of us thought it would. Five dead women . . . we're looking at a serial killer. I hope Angela didn't find herself in his crosshairs."

"It's not only that, but it sounds like all of you are in danger. Men coming to the house with torches? That's no joke. And with no reliable police department to call? You're in a bad situation."

I shivered again as I remembered it. "I know. Believe me, I know."

"Maybe you should just come home."

The thought of being home with him was very

tempting but . . . "If everybody left this case alone then there would be no justice for these girls."

"We don't want to add anyone else to this list of victims, especially you."

I suppose it was now or never that I was going to tell him. "Riley, Grayson Tech was bought out, and in a month I'm not going to have a job."

I blurted it without any filter. I knew if I tried to say it too nicely, I may not even get the news out or I'd end up sounding like I was reciting something I'd heard online.

"What? Are you for real?" Surprise lilted his voice.

I dropped down on my bed, exhausted from the weight of losing my job and delaying sharing the information. I should have just told him from the start. "Painfully so. I got the call yesterday, but I just couldn't bring myself to tell you. I'm sorry, Riley."

"There's no need to apologize. I'm sorry to hear about this. How are you holding up?"

I should've known that Riley would be concerned for me first and foremost. It was very sweet of him.

"I'm holding up okay." I pulled a pillow to my chest. "Of course, it's all a shock still. I don't know what exactly I'm going to do."

"You'll figure out something."

"Thanks for your confidence in me. But I know this affects you also, and I am really sorry about that. I knew you were thinking about quitting your job at the law firm and going out on your own." It would be easier when I had a steady income.

"Well, nothing's off the table yet. We'll figure it all out. As long as we have each other, we're going to be okay, right?"

I smiled, immediately comforted at his words. "Yes, you're right. Thanks for always believing in me."

"I love you, Gabby."

"I love you too, Riley."

I ended my day much better than I ever anticipated possible.

---

George joined us for breakfast the next morning. We were all tense and quiet as we sat there, enjoying our biscuits and gravy. Except none of us were really enjoying the food, even though it was certainly delicious. I sensed that each of us had things on our minds.

I wondered if Helene had changed her mind about us staying. If she regretted her words from last night. One look in her eyes, and I knew she hadn't.

But that led me to the question of whether or not we should leave anyway. The resounding answer in my mind was yes. But I needed to think everything through, to weigh the risks and benefits.

Those men had given us twenty-four hours before

they threatened to retaliate again. That meant we still had at least twelve hours to make our decision.

Finally, after several minutes of silence, I cleared my throat. "If you don't mind me asking, is there anyone here in town you think might be capable of murder?"

Helene and George glanced at each other. I knew my words had been stark, but I wanted to see their reaction.

I decided maybe I should explain a little bit more. "As I'm sure you both know, the body of a dead woman was discovered in the park about a month ago. Angela Vance, the woman we're looking for, was seen with this woman before she disappeared. We need to know if there was a connection between the dead woman and this town."

No one said anything for a moment. So I waited. Sometimes, silence was the best motivator to get people to talk. Usually, I remembered that when I was questioning someone whom I thought was guilty. That wasn't the case this time, but still I gave them a moment to compose their thoughts.

"The people in this town are protective of one another." George set his fork on his plate. "That doesn't make any of them a killer."

"But what about the men who came here last night and threatened to torch your house?" Evie asked, a touch of outrage in her voice. "You don't think they're capable of violence?"

"I didn't say I didn't think they were capable of

violence." George frowned. "I just don't know if they're capable of cold-blooded murder."

"Are you sure about that?" I asked. "Because men who are that brazen in one area of their lives are usually that brazen in all areas."

"I can't speak for them. Sure, they're bullies. I just don't want to think that anyone I personally know is capable of something like that."

"What about the police chief?" Duncan Cruiser was still on my radar. There was something about that man that got under my skin, and it was more than the fact that he was willing to overlook crimes that happened in his town.

"He's a piece of work," Helene wiped her mouth. She'd actually sat at the table to join us, and I was glad that she'd included herself. "Never have I ever liked him. He's good for nothing."

"How did he get to be police chief?" Sherman asked.

"He was appointed by the mayor, who just happens to be his cousin," Helene said.

"Is there anyone not related that would even be eligible?" I asked.

"I do believe there was one other person who was interested," George said. "I've only heard that through the grapevine, though. I wasn't in this area at that time."

"Who was this person?" I asked, unsure if this was related or useful even—but I really wanted to know.

"His name is William Manners."

There was a name I hadn't heard before. "What can you tell us about this William Manners guy?"

"There's not much to tell about him." George shrugged. "He grew up in this area, left for college, worked on Wall Street, and made a good amount of money for himself. He retired before he was fifty years old and moved back to his hometown to settle down."

That hadn't been the story I'd been expecting to hear, but it was interesting, nonetheless. "Anything else you know about him?"

"I know he had some kind of a rift with the Cruiser family many years ago. But he's not the type who backs down either."

He sounded like someone I might want to talk to. "Where can I find this guy?"

"I'm not sure where he lives," George said. "But if you see a man riding around town on a motorcycle, that's your guy."

# CHAPTER
## TWENTY-ONE

WE MET in Evie's room to discuss the case. She had some information she wanted to share with us.

She paced the room as Sherman and I sat on the edge of the bed watching. I brought a pen and paper so I could take notes.

"I've been reviewing the victims. There are similarities between them. They were each in their twenties or thirties. All of them were loners who had bad family lives they left behind. In other words, most of them had no one to look for them when they went missing."

I nodded and jotted down the information.

"There wasn't enough of a correlation there or even enough similarities physically for me to profile a type of victim this killer might target," Evie continued. "Each of these victims were last seen in different places."

I'd noticed this in the case files, but I let her continue,

sensing that saying this out loud helped her to make sense of things.

"Two of the victims were last seen on the Hanging Hill Highway," she continued. "One was hitchhiking there. The other was seen driving that way. Two other victims were seen in local businesses near the highway —one in a diner and the other at a gas station. None of the witnesses saw anything particular."

"And the last victim?" Sherman asked.

"That's our Jane Doe. She was last seen here in Shady Valley." Evie drew in a deep breath. "And this leads me to my profile of the killer. Knowing what I know now, I have a better picture of who this man is."

I swallowed hard, anxious to hear what she else had to say.

"This man is someone who likes control. It's obvious by the way the bodies were left. He didn't want anyone to stumble across them accidentally. No, he left these bodies where they'd be found on his terms."

Her words made sense. I waited for her to continue, scribbling more notes as I did.

"He's also someone who's an emotional killer. Sure, he wants to send a message. But the fact that he's strangled these women shows me that he has deep-seated issues. Maybe he was rejected and he needs to take vengeance on someone else. I don't know for sure yet."

"Insightful," Sherman said.

"He's probably a white male, and this guy probably

blends into whatever community he's part of," Evie said. "Otherwise, he would have been spotted in places like here in Shady Valley. People here notice everyone out of the ordinary. A guy leaving a body in the park? Someone would have noticed."

I shivered. She was right, though. This guy could be staring us in the face, and we just didn't know it.

"One other thing I found interesting . . ." Evie frowned. "The victims were always found on Thursdays."

How did that fit? I didn't know, but I would keep it in mind.

She paused. "That's all I have so far."

"That's really helpful," I said. "Thanks."

As we wrapped up our meeting, my phone rang. I looked down and saw that it was Daniel with the state police. I wondered what he was calling about now. I excused myself and stepped into the hallway so I could take the call.

"Hi, Daniel. Wasn't expecting to hear from you again so soon."

"Hey, Gabby. I wasn't expecting to have to call you again. But we just got a break, and I thought I owed it to you to tell you what we found."

I held my breath in anticipation of what he might say. "I appreciate any information that you're willing to share. What's going on?"

"A biker was out on the highway this morning. He

pulled off onto a back road and subsequently crashed. As he was walking, trying to find a cell phone signal, he found a car hidden in the woods."

My heart pounded harder. "Okay . . ."

"Any guesses as to who this car belongs to?"

"One of the victims, maybe."

"No, not exactly. I looked up the VIN number, and it turns out it's registered to one Angela Vance."

---

Evie, Sherman, and I picked up the rental car from the garage, dropped it off at the bed-and-breakfast, and then took off toward Harrisburg. It might be a good idea to get away from this town for a while anyway.

Evie looked especially pale beside me. Sherman reached into the front seat and squeezed her shoulder. Again, Evie didn't turn him away. Normally, her pride seemed to dictate her actions.

I hated that it had taken an event like this to soften up her tough façade. I knew not to push too hard and to let her have her moments of quiet. When she wanted to speak, she would. She needed to do things on her terms.

An hour later, we pulled into the State Police Department office in Harrisburg. Daniel met us inside, signed us in at the front desk, and led us toward the back of the building.

I quickly introduced him to my friends, and he

handed us his business card and insisted we all call him Daniel. Daniel was in his mid-forties, looked like a body builder, and boasted a bald head. He looked tough, but he was one of the nicest guys I'd met through my work.

"Maybe you all can help shed some light on this vehicle," he said.

I had no idea what—if anything—had been inside, if there was any evidence of a crime, or, even worse, if there had been any signs of foul play found, like blood.

I prayed that wasn't the case. But I couldn't stop wondering how the car had ended up on a mountain road twenty minutes from Shady Valley. What exactly had happened in the time Angela had left the area until this car was found?

"There are several things about the vehicle that makes it a little strange," Daniel said.

We stepped into the garage and saw a burgundy midsized sedan parked there. A few scratches showed on the side of the car, but otherwise everything looked surprisingly okay at first glance.

"Usually, when we find a vehicle in the woods like we did, there are indications that there was an accident." Daniel paced toward the vehicle. "Maybe someone veered off the road. But, in this case, there were hardly any scratches on the vehicle or any indications that there had been an incident of any sort."

I glanced at Evie, and I could see that she was soaking in all this information. I supposed that was a good sign. Part of me had feared that Angela was in an accident and had been unconscious for an indefinite amount of time before she'd ultimately . . . I frowned, not wanting to finish that thought.

"Was there anything inside to indicate what might've happened?" Evie finally asked, a slight tremble in her voice.

When I saw Daniel's frown, I braced myself for whatever he was about to say.

# CHAPTER
# TWENTY-TWO

"THE INSIDE WAS ALSO SURPRISINGLY CLEAN," Daniel said. "There was nothing to indicate foul play."

I released the breath I'd held. The update didn't necessarily give us answers, but it was good news.

"We've already gone through everything in the car," Daniel said. "So you can feel free to take a look. I hope you're able to find something and figure out what happened to your mom."

With a respectful nod, Daniel walked back inside and gave us a moment.

Though I wanted to take the lead, I let Evie slip into the driver's seat.

If it didn't look like it had been an accident, did that mean that Angela had pulled into the woods and had hidden the vehicle herself? And, if that was the

case, why would she do that? Had she gone somewhere on foot afterward or had somebody picked
her up?

We still had so many questions.

Finally, Evie got out and turned toward us. "I didn't
see anything inside that gave any indication of what
might have happened. It's great that we found her car,
but I'm not sure how much we can do with this."

"At least there are no signs that she was injured,"
Sherman said.

Evie nodded. "You're right. That is good news."

"Do you mind?" I pointed to the driver's seat. "I'd
like to take a look at the vehicle."

"Please. Go right ahead," Evie said.

I slipped behind the steering wheel. As I glanced
around, I imagined Angela sitting here. I imagined her
pulling into the woods, parking the car, and getting out.
Her keys weren't found in the vehicle, which led me to
believe that Angela had left on her own.

What if she had somehow followed the distraught
woman who had left from Pumpernickels? Hillary had
said Angela had gone after the girl. What if this girl had
gotten in a car with somebody, taken off down the road,
and Angela had decided to trail after them?

I wasn't sure how much validity my theory had, but
at least it was something.

I glanced around again, looking for something—
anything—that the police might have missed. But if

Daniel said he hadn't seen anything out of the ordinary, there was a little chance I would find something either.

Finally, I climbed out. "I'd like to find out where this car was discovered and then go check out that area ourselves."

"I think that sounds like a great idea," Evie said.

At least we were all in agreement.

---

Twenty minutes later, I was driving down what appeared, despite its morbid name, to be a peaceful mountain road. Hanging Hill Highway was a sight to see. Leaves were just popping out fresh on the trees and looking green and vibrant. A little stream trickled beside us. Everything appeared so serene, even though nothing about this situation seemed to agree with the sentiment.

"What exactly do you think we might find?" Sherman popped his head between us in the front seat.

"I don't know." I tightened my jaw, praying I'd say the right thing. "We may not find anything. But at least we'll have a better idea of where Angela was."

"I feel like I should be happy that her car was found." Evie stared out the window, her voice as dull as her gaze. "But it seems that I feel more unsettled than ever. Why would Angela leave her car in the woods like that? And the fact that she never returned to her car doesn't feel right."

My gut twisted at her words. I knew if we pushed hard enough, we might be able to initiate a search effort. We could get a couple of canines and see if they could follow Angela's scent, but I feared too much time had passed.

I glanced at my phone. I had put in the GPS coordinates, and I knew we were close. As a British voice instructed, I pulled off to the side of the road. We were here.

I put my car in Park and turned to my team. "This is it. Ready to check things out?"

"Let's just get this over with," Evie mumbled.

We stepped outside. I hadn't been able to park right at the scene because the road was too narrow. Instead, we walked along the asphalt shoulder on the scattered gravel there. On the other side of the road, a stream babbled.

Or did it warn us away?

And the birds overhead that squawked . . . they were almost like guardians who knew we were intruders here. They almost sounded like they were alerting anyone close by that we were coming.

I scanned everything around us, looking for the area where Angela's car had been. We should be able to spot the trampled underbrush.

Finally, about fifteen feet into our walk, I paused.

This had to be it.

The foliage looked disturbed, and there was just

enough room for a vehicle to pull between the trees. Broken branches littered the area.

Daniel had said that branches had been placed over the car, so that it wasn't easily visible from the road. Those branches were the only reason no one had discovered the car before. Right now, they looked shriveled and frail, like they were embarrassed about what they had done.

We observed the area for a moment in silence. What exactly had Angela been thinking when she left her car here? And why here, of all places? Or maybe she hadn't left it here at all. Maybe someone else had concealed her car.

I looked around on either side of me. A gravel road stretched both ways, no doubt leading to some secluded residences in the area. Nothing else was around here.

But this area had to be significant in some way.

Evie held up her phone. "If Angela stopped out here, she probably didn't have a signal."

Sherman held up his phone also. "If I lean to the left, I can get one bar. But you're probably right. Service is spotty."

Out of curiosity, I carefully walked within a six-foot perimeter of the broken branches. I knew the police had examined the car and the place where it was found, but I wanted to see if there was anything in the area that they might have missed. It was a long shot, but it was worth trying.

Something caught in the brush grabbed my attention. I paced over to it and squatted down for a better look. Pulling my sleeve over my hand, I reached down and picked the object up. I needed to be careful not to ruin any evidence, just in case this was significant.

"What is it?" Evie walked toward me.

I held up my find. "This is a tobacco pouch. And if I'm not mistaken, it's the same kind that Chief Cruiser chews."

We exchanged a look, but none of us had to say anything to realize the implication.

"We need to give that to Lt. Yoder," Sherman said.

Yes, we did. Because I didn't like the conclusions that came together in my mind.

Still gripping the tobacco pouch with my sleeve, I took a step back toward the road. Hopefully, I could find something in my car to put this in until we got back to the state police office.

But as I stepped toward the road, a new figure appeared from seemingly nowhere.

Chief Cruiser stood in front of us, fisting and unfisting his hands. But that wasn't what scared me the most. No, it was the look of vengeance in his eyes that shook me down to my bones.

# CHAPTER
## TWENTY-THREE

"THIS ISN'T what it looks like," Cruiser growled. His eyes looked dilated, and sweat beaded across his skin, despite the chilly temperatures.

I took a step back, wishing more than anything that I had brought my gun with me. But I hadn't. I could now see that was a grave mistake.

"How'd you find us here?" My neck stiffened as adrenaline surged through me.

"I was patrolling the area when I saw you and decided to see what you were up to. I followed you here. I needed to know what you were up to."

"Would you care to explain why you wanted to do that?" I kept myself between Cruiser and my friends. At least they'd have a head start if we needed to run.

"I didn't hurt that woman." Cruiser said the words, but his lips barely moved. He had all the signs of being on the verge of a psychotic break . . . or quite possibly going crazy on us.

We were face-to-face right now with a potential killer with no backup plan and no lifeline. The only good news was that there were three of us against one of him. The bad news was that he had a gun.

"If you didn't hurt that woman, how did your tobacco pouch get here?" I hardened my voice, trying to sound tougher than I actually was.

"I was investigating." The chief's mustache twitched.

I didn't bother to hide the humor from my voice. "Good one."

"I was," he said. "I was trying to find out what happened."

"And what did you find out?" Evie's voice sounded icy cold with determination as she stepped forward, her tight muscles looking poised for a fight.

"Nothing." He spit some tobacco juice onto the ground. "I didn't find out anything."

I ignored how absolutely disgusting his habit was and focused on Angela. "So you just left Angela's car here and failed to report it? Not very professional."

"It's complicated." His lips twitched down a frown.

"You know who says that?" I asked. "People who are guilty and trying to justify their actions. I've seen it one million times before."

"It's not like that."

"Then why did you follow us here?" I asked. "What are you planning on doing now?"

Part of me didn't want to hear his answer, but I had to know just how much danger we were in. Maybe then I could figure out how we would get out of this.

"Because I knew you were getting close to answers. I had to see how close."

"Why don't we all go down to the State Police Department and talk there?" I suggested. "Doesn't that sound like a good idea?"

"We don't need to bring them into this." Cruiser stepped toward me, his nostrils flaring.

"Again, another indication of guilt." The words rolled off my tongue dryly. I didn't want to anger him. I really didn't. But this man was the epitome of everything I couldn't stand.

"I am not guilty." Cruiser's voice turned steely hard.

"What do you think we should do right now?" I asked.

"I don't know." His voice rose along with his emotion. If we weren't careful, he would blow his top.

"I suggest you think a little faster, because I don't plan on staying out here all day," I said. "We don't have much longer to find answers, and we don't appreciate being held up."

"I just need that evidence." The chief's voice came out at a low growl.

He reached for the pouch of tobacco, but I pulled back. "No way."

His eyes narrowed even more. "Don't make this harder than it has to be."

At that moment, I heard a siren chirp behind us. The next instant, a State Police SUV squealed to a stop on the road behind Cruiser, and Daniel strode toward us.

I glanced back at my friends. How in the world had he known to come? I didn't even care right now. I was just glad he was here.

"Just the man I was looking for," Daniel said, grabbing Cruiser's arm. "Let's go to the station and have a chat."

Cruiser scowled at us. "We were just talking. I didn't do nothing wrong."

"We'll be the judge of that." Daniel ushered him into the back of the car, Cruiser back talking the entire time.

I glanced back at my friends again. Certainly, the relief on their faces reflected my own expression. If Daniel hadn't show up when he did . . .

"How did Daniel know to come?" I asked.

"As soon as we found the tobacco bag, I thought we should let the proper authorities know," Sherman said. "I found a spot with reception and texted Daniel. Then I sent him an SOS as soon as I saw this guy show up. He just happened to be headed toward Shady Valley. If he hadn't been close, I don't know how things would have turned out."

"Smart thinking," I said.

"I do that sometimes." He flashed a smile.

"I'd say you do that all the time." Evie offered a grateful smile.

I whispered a prayer of thanks for God's provision. I couldn't wait to find out what this guy had to say, nor could I wait to give Daniel this tobacco pouch.

My thoughts were somber as I walked down the road, careful to remain on the side. We'd made some strides, but we still needed more answers.

Even if Cruiser was guilty, where was Angela?

I hoped Daniel could get that information from him.

"That was a close one, huh?" Sherman said. "I still can't get over it."

I nodded when I remembered seeing Cruiser standing there, when I'd realized he'd followed us. "Yes, it was. Again, smart thinking letting Daniel know."

"My gut tells me that Angela is out here some- where." Evie glanced at the vast wilderness around us.

"In these woods?" I clarified.

She nodded, a hollow look in her eyes. "Yes, in these woods. I don't know why, but I think she parked there and took off."

My gut told me the same thing. "Daniel will figure something out."

The last thing we needed to do was take off, looking by ourselves. Not only would it take forever to gain any ground, but there was also the possibility of getting lost. We needed a lot of people to perform that kind of search.

I reached down and picked up a paper from the ground. Another way of leaving the world a little better than I'd found it. That's what the book told me, at least.

Out of curiosity, I opened the folded white paper, expecting to find a flyer or an advertisement.

Instead, I saw a printed photo of someone who looked strangely like William Manners, only younger.

I sucked in a breath.

"What is it?" Evie asked

I showed her what I'd found. "This can't be a coincidence."

Evie frowned. "No, it can't."

"I wonder if this somehow fell out of Angela's car as it was being towed," I said.

"It's a possibility . . ." Evie's gaze was still narrowed with thought. "But why would Angela have his picture? I don't understand."

"I have no idea."

Evie frowned. "From the sound of it, Angela didn't come to Shady Valley looking for the woman she saw in Pumpernickels. She came here looking for someone else, and she just happened to stumble upon a serial killer in the process."

# CHAPTER
# TWENTY-FOUR

MY FRIENDS and I waited in the lobby at the state police station. It wasn't how I wanted to spend the rest of my day, especially considering how little time we had left. We were supposed to pack up and leave tomorrow, and I had little hope we would have answers before then.

That was, unless Chief Cruiser fessed up while he was talking to Daniel. I had a feeling that wouldn't happen. But I also knew that Daniel could break the most determined of criminals. Stories of his tenacity had come out when I'd had lunch with the crew the last time I was here doing a workshop. His colleagues had bragged on him.

We were all hungry, so we grabbed some snacks from the vending machine. Barbecue chips for me, a candy bar for Sherman, and some trail mix for Evie.

As we munched, I turned to my friends. "So, what do you think? Is Cruiser involved?"

"That's what all the evidence points to," Evie said. "Why else would he have followed Angela here? I'm guessing he stalked her here and maybe chased her through the woods."

"Then why doesn't Angela's disappearance fit the details of the rest of these cases in the area?" Sherman said. "Something is different about it, and I can't figure out what changed."

"My guess is that she got pulled into something," I offered, popping a chip in my mouth. "That she tried to help and somehow found herself in the middle of this. The question is, where is she now?"

"We need cadaver dogs." Evie's voice cracked.

"You don't really think . . ." I couldn't bring myself to finish my question.

"At this point, I don't know what to think. But, if I'm being honest, that is the most likely explanation as to what happened."

I didn't say anything. I knew her words were true. There was a good chance that Angela's body was lying out there somewhere in the mountains. It would take weeks to search for it. And, even if she was out there, there was a good possibility she would never be found.

We sat in silence for a minute, each mulling over our own thoughts. Finally, the door leading to the office area opened and Daniel stepped out. "Can I see you all in the conference room for a moment?"

Anxiety stretched through the air as we threw our trash away and followed him into the room. We each took a seat at the table there. This is where I'd done my workshop when I'd come. It felt much different being here now.

"We've just spent the past two hours questioning Cruiser." Daniel looked at each of us from his place at the head of the table. "I don't believe he has anything to do with the disappearance of your mother, Evie. I am sorry to tell you that."

"But what about his tobacco?" Evie's voice rose with emotion.

"We confirmed initially that it is his tobacco, and he admitted that he did come to the site. That doesn't prove his guilt, however."

"Why else would he be at the site if he wasn't involved in the crime?" Evie's voice rose, and she pressed her hands into the table.

"He admits that he followed Angela when she left town. He saw her pull off, so he turned around and went back into town. When the dead body was found two days later, he went back to the same area to see if he could find out where Angela had gone. She was the last person seen with our Jane Doe. Instead, he found Angela's empty car."

"What happened next?" Sherman crossed his arms,

looking impatient as he tapped his finger against his bicep. And Sherman never looked impatient. "Did you ask him why he didn't investigate it further?"

"It appears he dropped the investigation. He said all his leads dried up and there was nothing else he could do."

"He's dirty," I muttered.

"I believe he is also," Daniel agreed. "In fact, we have him in custody for corruption. He won't be going back to police work, at least not until we do a thorough investigation."

"Where does that leave us with the search for Angela?" Evie's voice changed from charged to sounding paper thin and fragile. She seemed to notice and rubbed her throat.

Daniel hesitated a moment and folded his hands together in front of him. "All of this is confidential. You can't repeat it. The only reason I'm sharing this is because I know Gabby's reputation. I've only heard good things about you two also."

I held my breath, waiting to hear what he would have to say and feeling in my gut that this would be a turning point.

Daniel leaned forward, still looking intense. "It finally came out that Cruiser believes his uncle might be behind these crimes."

I sucked in a breath. "His uncle? You mean Big Frankie?"

"He's the one."

"That would explain where his wife got that necklace that supposedly belonged to a dead girl," Evie said.

"Cruiser doesn't have any evidence that this is true. He just suspects it is. He was trying to find answers, and he ended up brushing most of this case under the rug as a result."

"And there's where the corruption comes in," I muttered.

Daniel nodded. "Exactly. I'm going to send some guys out to bring Big Frankie in. I want to talk to him and hear his story myself. Thanks so much for all your help."

"I know it's probably too much to ask, but I would love to hear if there are any more updates." I waited for his response, hoping I wasn't pressing my luck.

Daniel nodded. "I'll share what I can. But again, I need your discretion."

"You've got it," I told him. "Discretion is my middle name."

We went back to the bed-and-breakfast. Helene and George were outside feeding the horses when we arrived. We gave them an update, telling them what we could, but careful to keep quiet what was confidential.

Those men from last night had threatened to return

in four hours. However, with Chief Cruiser and Big Frankie potentially behind bars, maybe most of the danger was no longer an issue. I could hope, at least.

"What now?" Evie said as we stood in the hallway between our rooms.

"At this point, I don't think it's going to do any good to question any more people here in town," I said. "Part of me thinks we just need to wait to hear what Daniel and his crew find out. If Big Frankie is behind this, maybe he has the answers we need."

"But what if he doesn't have the answers?" Evie crossed her arms, a challenging look in her eyes.

She had a point. We needed to explore every possibility while we were here.

"You know, you're right," I said. "Until we hear something definite, we should keep digging. After all, we have until the end of the day tomorrow to give it everything we've got. After that, I know we each have to get back to our everyday lives."

"I need to go check my emails," Sherman said. "I put out some feelers, and I want to see if I got any hits yet."

"Go right ahead," I said, wondering what he put out feelers on.

I had only just stepped into my room and tried to put together my thoughts when Sherman called to us. With curiosity adding a spring to my steps, I rushed into his room and waited. He sat at a little desk in the corner, his computer in front of him and a smile on his face.

"You'll never believe this," he said. "I did a facial recognition search online for our Jane Doe. I knew it was a long shot and that I most likely wouldn't get any hits. But I did."

I sucked in a breath. "That's great news. What did you find out?"

"I found out that our Jane Doe might possibly be someone named Megan Gurski." He turned the screen toward us, and a smiling face stared back.

I studied the image there. I could see where the match was possible. But I wanted to hear more.

"She fits the profile that we put together." Sherman pushed his glasses up higher. "She was from West Virginia, but she left home. Her parents were both druggies, and she was somewhat of a drifter."

"So you think she came here?" Evie asked. "And then Angela just happened to run into her?"

"I feel like there are still details that we're missing, but essentially yes, that's what I am wondering."

I nodded slowly, feeling like the theory had merit. "It's a start. But Sherman, how is it that you were able to find a match on this girl when the police haven't yet?"

Sherman shrugged. "I've actually been working as a contractor for Homeland Security and developing this program. The details have all been hush-hush, and it hasn't been released yet. But I decided to try it on this Jane Doe, and it looks like it worked."

"That's great news," Evie said. "Good work, Sherman."

"Thanks." Sherman practically glowed at her affirmation.

He had it bad. Really, really bad. And I feared his heart might just get broken beyond repair.

# CHAPTER
# TWENTY-FIVE

WHILE SHERMAN KEPT SEARCHING for more information and hits online to see if our victims were connected in some way, I decided to look a little more into this woman he had discovered. Evie also escaped into her room and said she was going to do some work as well. Maybe each of us just needed a bit of time to ourselves.

Evie knocked at my door around seven p.m. A new light filled her eyes. "I think I know the connection."

She motioned for Sherman and me to come into her room. We all bent over a map she had laid out on her bed. Little red marks stretched along part of it.

"This is a map of Pennsylvania," she started. "I marked the locations where each of the victims were found dead. We were looking for a commonality, right?

Look what runs right in the center of each of the death scenes."

I leaned closer to look at where she was pointing and sucked in a breath.

"It's the highway," she muttered.

Evie was right. The highway where we'd found Angela's car was ground zero for these missing women. All of them had been found within a few miles of Hanging Hill.

"So what connects all these women isn't necessarily age or a certain look or a certain social position, but it's an area," I muttered.

Evie raised her head and nodded. "Bingo."

"So somehow this Megan Gurski ended up on the highway," I continued. "Angela must've gone after her. Maybe she even saw something happen and pulled her car over to either follow someone or to help. And that's where the trouble started."

"My thoughts exactly."

Sherman glanced at his watch. "Guys, not to rain on your parade here, but it's getting close to the deadline those punks gave us. What do you think we should do?"

"Helene made it clear that she thinks we should stay." Evie crossed her arms. "But I obviously don't want to put her in danger or bring her any more trouble."

"I was thinking about that," I said. "However, since

Chief Cruiser's behind bars and Big Frankie should be in custody, I think we should be okay."

Sherman and Evie offered a hesitant nod.

"But if you think we should leave, I'm okay with doing that," I continued, torn about what the right thing was.

"I don't want to hear anything more about it."

We all turned as a new voice came to the door. Helene stood there. She'd obviously heard the last part of our conversation.

"It's like I said last night, I will not make my decisions based on pressure from bullies," she said. "I don't know what's going on or what the police are working on. Frankly, I don't really care. I just know that my decision has been made and you all are staying here. Understand?"

The stern tone of her voice left no room for questions. We all nodded.

"Good. I fixed dinner. I know you don't usually eat here in the evening, but I'd be honored if you'd share a meal with me. I made my famous chicken and dumplings, and you're not going to want to miss them."

"That sounds great," I said. "What time?"

"Fifteen minutes," Helene said.

Perfect. That would give me just enough time to call Daniel.

I left Evie's room and closed the door to my own room. I wasted no time dialing Daniel's number and giving him the update. He thanked me, said we'd done good work, and promised to look into it.

"There's something I think you should know," Daniel said after I finished.

Based on his tone, that wasn't a good thing. "What's going on?"

"We went to bring in Big Frankie," Daniel said. "But he's missing."

My heart rate quickened. "What do you mean, missing?"

"I mean, we haven't been able to find him. He's on the run."

"I might know where he's going."

I filled him in on what happened last night.

But I didn't like the sound of this. If my calculations were correct, that man should be showing up here in an hour.

---

I tried to enjoy my food. I really did. Helene was a great cook, and I had a feeling she missed having people to prepare food for, people who would appreciate her hard work. Sherman, Evie, George, and I sat around the table and made small talk. But my mind wouldn't leave what Daniel had told me about Big Frankie. Where exactly had the man gone, and what was he planning?

I tried not to keep glancing at the time on my smart

watch, but I failed. Those men had showed up here last night at eight. I wondered if that was the time they would show up again tonight, or if they even *would* show up tonight. I had been pretty confident that they wouldn't, but now that Big Frankie was in the wind, I wondered if it might still be a possibility.

My watch told me we had only five minutes until we would find out. And, though no one said anything, I had a feeling the same thing was on each of our minds.

Just as Helene stepped out with an apple dump cake, I heard tires on the gravel out front. My spine stiffened.

Someone was here.

I looked at my friends, then at George and Helene. "Maybe we should all get away from the windows."

Part of me wanted to tell them to run. Getting away from the windows would do nothing if these guys threw torches into the house.

George grabbed the gun he'd left in the corner. "No way am I going to hide."

Helene stepped up next to him. "And neither am I."

Though I admired their bravery, I really didn't want to see either of them get hurt. I didn't want to see *anyone* get hurt. But I had no idea how this was going to turn out.

As George and Helene stepped onto the porch, I followed them outside. Sherman and Evie joined me.

"What are you doing here?" George yelled, his gun pointed at the crowd.

I scanned the people here. It was the same men from last night, and there in the middle of all of them stood Big Frankie. Either he hadn't heard there was a warrant out for his arrest or he didn't care. I didn't know which possibility bothered me more.

"The deadline is up." Big Frankie sneered as he looked at us. "It looks like you've made your choice."

"Nobody is leaving." Helene's hands were fisted at her hips, her body language a sharp contrast to her plain, traditional dress and usually soft voice. "These people are my guests."

"And we told you when you moved here that we didn't like outsiders."

"And my husband, Tom, told you that we don't care," Helene said. "He fought for this country, and he fought to give people the freedoms that we take for granted. You aren't going to tell me what I can and cannot do here on my property."

"Very well then." Big Frankie raised the torch in his hands.

# CHAPTER
# TWENTY-SIX

A ZING of anxiety ripped through me. I stepped back, trying to shield my friends from the danger in front of us. I really didn't want things to end this way.

This house was old. It wouldn't take much for everything to catch fire. All of Helene's possessions could be gone in an instant.

"You had your chance," Big Frankie growled.

He pulled his arm back, as if preparing to launch the torch at the house. I held my breath.

Before he could, I heard footsteps scatter around us. "Police!"

Daniel's men charged from around the side of the house where they'd been hiding. All they'd needed was proof of a threat to make these arrests. There was clearly no doubt about what these men's intentions had been.

Relief filled me, and my shoulders drooped.

It had been risky letting it get this far, but Daniel had insisted this might be the only way we catch Big Frankie. And it had worked. Thankfully.

Three of his troopers surrounded the overgrown bully and cuffed his hands amidst his curses. The torches were snuffed out and all the men were led to police cars that had been hidden away in the barn.

It was over. We were okay. The bed-and-breakfast was still standing.

I put my arm around Helene. "You did good."

She ran a hand over her head, swiping back loose hair that had escaped from her bun. "I would've done the same thing whether the police had been here or not."

"I know you would have. Hopefully, Lt. Yoder and his guys will get some answers about what's going on here in this town."

"I can only hope so." Her voice trembled as she watched the men being led away. "Because I have lived like this for too long."

The next morning, we got the news that the state police were going to send out their dogs to see if they could pick up a trail on Angela Vance. According to Daniel, they didn't have expectations of finding anything, but they were going to give it a shot. I feared their mission was one of recovery instead of rescue. I kept that thought silent, though.

We were all scheduled to leave today, but Evie insisted she wanted to stay longer to see what they discovered.

I couldn't blame her. Even though I was supposed to do a workshop down in Richmond, Virginia, tomorrow, I planned on remaining here as long as I could. I'd figure the rest out later.

In the meantime, Big Frankie hadn't confessed to anything. He had told the police that he found the skull necklace on the ground and gave it to his wife. He had insisted that there was no crime in doing that and that he knew nothing about Megan Gurski.

I still felt that he was holding something back, and I hoped the police might get more from him today.

Even though we hadn't found Angela yet, we'd taken great strides in this case. We'd uncovered connection about the deaths of five women, and we were closer than ever to finding the killer. We knew that Angela had intersected with one of the victims, but the fact that she hadn't been found indicated that she could still be alive.

I wished that we'd been able to get total closure and it wasn't too late. We just might not get that closure while we were here in Shady Valley.

We ate breakfast as normal with Helene and George. They both seemed a little more at peace than they had yesterday, and we'd even made casual chitchat before George hurried off to his part-time job.

After we ate, Evie, Sherman, and I headed back toward our rooms. As we went up the steps, Sherman's phone rang. He put it to his ear, his voice changing from serious to soft.

"Hey, you," he said. "That's right. I'm going to be headed back today. At least, that *was* the plan . . . Well, it's nice being missed . . . I heard that was a good restaurant also. I would love to go try it sometime."

A couple seconds later, he chuckled into the phone before ending his call and putting his phone away. He sounded happy. He had to be talking to the new girl at his office again. If he hadn't found love with Evie, at least he'd met this new woman.

Evie turned toward him, something flashing in her eyes. "I can't believe you would want to date someone like that."

"Someone like what?" A defensive edge crept into Sherman's voice. "You don't even know her."

"I don't have to know her to know that she's not your type at all."

Sherman crossed his arms, looking more irritated than I'd ever seen him, with his narrowed eyes and tight jaw. "And what exactly is my type?"

Evie rolled her eyes. "I don't know exactly, but not that."

I decided to step in and be the voice of reason. It was

a sad day when I had to be that person. "What is it about this woman that makes you think she's not Sherman's type, Evie?"

"She sounds ditzy," Evie finally said, raising her chin.

"She's not ditzy. She's nice and she's smart and she's pretty. You'd like her if you ever met her."

Evie's jaw twitched right before her face muscles went placid. "I see. I guess I should say I'm happy for you. You found what you wanted. I just hope she doesn't take you away from your career, because you've got too much to offer to be distracted by love."

With that, Evie stormed into her room and slammed her door.

I turned to Sherman and mouthed the word "sorry." That had been ugly. Really ugly.

He shrugged. "It's not your fault. But I don't understand her reaction. She's obviously not interested, and I thought I had given her all the right signals."

"Maybe she didn't think she was interested until she realized you might be off the market. Maybe hearing you talk to this other woman is making her realize that she does care for you."

He shrugged again. "Maybe. Or maybe she honestly doesn't see the point in relationships—not when you can be married to your career. Either way, women are so confusing. I would do anything for Evie. Yet I just feel like she resents me."

"I would say give her time, but . . ." But Evie was such a mystery to me. Just when I thought I'd figured her out, I hadn't.

"Yeah, I know." He shoved his hands into his pockets and paused. "Now what?"

Since he'd changed the subject . . . "There is one more thing I would like to do before we leave town. I want to go talk to William Manners."

"Why would you do that? Besides, Big Frankie is already in custody. And hasn't Daniel already talked to this William guy?"

"I'm not sure if he has or not. But I keep thinking about what Evie discovered about that highway. It seems to be the center of all of this. I know that this William guy mostly rides around all day on these roads. If Big Frankie isn't our guy, maybe William is. I know it's a long shot and that it might not matter. But, before I leave town, I would like to confirm that. Would you like to come?"

"I would love to. Give me two minutes, and I'll be right out."

While he went into his room, I knocked on Evie's door. A second later, she jerked it open and stared at me. If I didn't know better, I would think that she might've been crying. Her eyes looked red and glassy.

"What?" she barked. Her voice dared me to acknowledge what I saw, to voice aloud her weak moment.

I kept my expression even and my voice nonjudgmental. "Do you have a moment?"

"I guess."

She left the door open and walked away, which I accepted as an invitation. I took a step inside her room and closed the door behind me, but I didn't make a move to get any closer. I lingered there by the door, keeping my distance and watching as Evie organized some papers on her desk.

"Evie, I know this has been hard on you," I started. "I can't even imagine what you're going through—"

"No, you can't. No one can." She didn't bother to look at me. Instead, she continued to methodically straighten her papers.

"I just don't understand why you're lashing out at Sherman when all he's trying to do is help you."

"All he's doing is flaunting the fact that he has a girlfriend."

"I hardly think that talking to her on the phone means he's flaunting anything." I had to work really hard to keep my tone soft so I wouldn't stir up any unnecessary emotions.

She turned from her desk and glared at me. "Listen to how his voice changes. It's pathetic. I didn't think he was one of those guys. I thought he was stronger than that."

"Finding love isn't just for the weak, Evie."

"I never said it was." Her voice didn't sound convincing.

"You didn't have to."

She rolled her eyes. "I just don't see what the big deal is. I'm doing fine on my own."

"But are you?" I knew I was venturing into emotionally charged territory. "I mean, if that's true, then great. I'm really happy for you. But there's no shame in relying on other people. Life is lonely when you do it by yourself. But when you have people around you to help carry your burdens, it can be a blessing. It can help you keep your sanity and can give you strength to continue on your toughest days."

She said nothing, so I continued.

"I can say these things because I know about them firsthand. Evie, you know my story. You know what my childhood was like and what I've been through. Without my friends and without God . . . I would not be where I am today. They've only made me stronger."

"Are you done with your sermon now?"

Her words made me flinch as if I'd been slapped. I'd poured out my heart to her and tried to show her that I cared. But she was only pushing me away again. I knew not to take it personally. These were her issues, her emotions that simmered beneath the surface.

I swallowed hard, knowing there was nothing else I could say. "Look, Sherman and I are going to go back into town one last time, and we're going to try to talk to William Manners. Would you like to come with us?"

She remained quiet until finally shaking her head. "I think I need some time alone. If you don't mind, I'll stay here."

"Do you want me to drive you out to the scene when they let the dogs go?"

"I'm not sure. I'll think about it."

I nodded and stepped away, hating how somber I felt. "Very well then. Let us know if you need anything."

# CHAPTER
## TWENTY-SEVEN

SHERMAN and I paused on the sidewalk and glanced around downtown Shady Valley. Numerous people were out on the streets right now. If I thought people had been hostile earlier, they were downright vicious now. The looks thrown at us could kill.

Clearly, no one wanted us to be here. But, after everything that had transpired, I doubted anybody would try to run us off—not now that the state police were involved and their chief of police was being held in custody.

"I have no idea how we should go about finding this William Manners guy," I told Sherman, keeping my head high despite the opposition around us. "I've seen him riding around on the streets at least three times, but I have no idea what his address is or how to locate him."

I could hear the mental clock ticking toward our deadline, and I knew we needed answers now.

I looked down the street and saw Hillary and her mom scurrying into Pumpernickels. They both cast us dirty looks as they did so. I had a feeling people were scurrying about, sharing the news about what had happened. Word of it seemed to be spreading faster than a clever meme on social media, and we were making even more enemies with every second that passed.

"I guess I shouldn't have expected to come here, stand on the sidewalk, and think this guy would somehow show up," I told Sherman.

"No, it probably wasn't the best game plan we've ever had."

I backed up and leaned against the building for a moment, closing my eyes. I still couldn't believe everything that had transpired since we'd arrived. It almost seemed surreal, like some kind of movie was playing out in front of us. But, instead, this was all reality. A terrible, terrible reality.

"How much time should we give this?" Sherman glanced at the time on his smart watch.

"That's a great question. I don't suppose this is doing any good, is it? We are just wasting time. I guess we should get back and talk to Evie."

Just as I said the words, I heard a sound down the street. I froze. It couldn't be . . . could it?

In slow motion, I turned my head toward the noise. I let out a breath of relief when I spotted William Manners headed down the street on his motorcycle. Perfect timing.

He passed us, turning his head slightly in acknowledgment. I waved my hands and ran after him. "Wait!"

He kept going. Of course.

When he rounded the corner, I stopped and shook my head.

That hadn't worked out the way I wanted.

I could rush to my car and chase after him. But I knew I'd be too far behind.

Instead, I bit down and scolded myself, feeling the opportunity slip through my hands.

But what I really wanted to know was why William Manners' picture was found on the road not far from Angela's car. That man was somehow connected, and I wanted to know how.

Sherman and I walked back to my car, my steps slower this time.

"At least we tried, I suppose." There were so many ways I should have handled that differently, I needed to figure out how to remedy it.

As I stepped toward my car, a footstep sounded behind us. I froze again, expecting trouble. Halfway expecting a man with a torch.

Instead, when I looked up, I saw William Manners standing there.

"You're looking for me?" His icy eyes bore into mine.

"As a matter fact, we are."

"What for?"

"We have a few questions for you." I gripped my keys and prepared to use them as a weapon if necessary. My throat burned as I realized this could be a dangerous situation. "Do you mind?"

"Depends on what it's about."

"You said you saw this woman." I found Angela's picture on my phone. "But what aren't you telling us?"

The man's lips pulled down as he looked off into the distance. "Maybe there was more to our conversation than I let on."

"Like what?" I demanded. "You know this is a life-or-death situation, right?"

"I didn't know everything then that I know now."

"What does that mean?" Why couldn't I get a straight answer from this guy?

William's gaze locked on mine. "What I mean is that Angela Vance is my sister."

The air left my lungs. Had I just heard him correctly?

"She's your sister?" Sherman repeated, a dumbfounded look on his face.

William's lip twitched again before he let out a sigh. He shifted, his thick boots thudding on the asphalt.

Finally, his eyes met mine again. "That's right. I believe she came here looking for me."

This whole time I figured Angela had been here looking for Megan. But I'd been totally wrong. I couldn't wait to hear what else this guy had to say.

"Would you care to expound on that?" All my senses tingled as I realized just how close answers could be.

He shifted, holding his bike helmet to his hip. "I was adopted by a family on the outskirts of town when I was ten. I had a little sister who was only a year old when we were put into the foster care system."

Now that he said that, I remembered that Angela Vance had been a product of the foster care system herself. It was one of the reasons she had felt so strongly about being a foster mom.

I waited for him to continue.

"I never saw my sister again. The records were closed, and I suppose I should've looked harder. But circumstances weren't ideal, and I didn't have a lot of resources. But after I went to college and got my career going, I decided I was going to see what I could find out. Again, my search led to a lot of dead ends. I didn't think I was going to find her."

"So how did Angela end up here looking for you?" I asked. "How did she find you?"

"My guess? Partially by accident." He pressed his lips together. "Like I said, she *did* find me. She asked me about that girl. When she talked to me, our eyes met, and I had a feeling I knew her. I just couldn't place her. I think she felt the same way."

"And then?" I pictured it all playing out in my mind, but I retained a good dose of skepticism, just to be safe.

"As she started running down the sidewalk trying to find this girl, she called out that she would like to talk to me again while she was here in town. I had no idea what she wanted to talk about. I was about to tell her I was married, but before I could, she was gone. After that moment, I kept thinking about her. That's when I realized who she was. I began doing my research again, and it confirmed that Angela Vance is my biological sister."

"And you just found this out?" I questioned, wondering why he didn't seem more invested.

He frowned and lowered his gaze. "That's correct. It takes time to hear back from people to confirm it. Once I knew for sure, I didn't want to stir up trouble where there didn't need to be trouble. The good Lord knows there's enough trouble in this town as it is. Last thing I wanted was to paint myself in a suspicious light when it came to her disappearance. But now I want to do anything I can to help."

"How can we know that you're telling the truth?" I couldn't take this guy at his word. Why should I? I knew nothing about him.

"If you'd like, I can send you all the documents that will prove that Angela and I are related."

"Yes, I would like you to do that."

Everything we'd learned turned over in my head. If he had been telling the truth, then we did have a lot more answers now than we did earlier. But it also meant that William Manners probably wasn't our bad guy.

That meant that either Duncan Cruiser or Big Frankie were lying . . . or we'd been looking in the wrong direction this whole time.

# CHAPTER
# TWENTY-EIGHT

WE GOT BACK to the bed-and-breakfast and rushed upstairs to share with Evie what we'd learned. But when I knocked on her door, it opened. I pushed it until I could see inside, unease snaking up my spine.

"Evie?"

No one answered. I glanced around, but the room was empty.

"She's not here," I told Sherman.

"I didn't see her downstairs either."

"Let's go talk to Helene. Maybe Evie told her something."

We went back downstairs and found the innkeeper in the kitchen baking cookies. I paused in front of her, ignoring the tantalizing scent of vanilla that filled the space.

"Hi, Helene," I started. "Sherman and I are looking for Evie. Have you seen her?"

"She left about an hour ago. Said she wanted to take a drive." Helene rolled out some dough on the counter, flour dusting every available surface.

Alarm raced through me. Why would Evie take a drive without telling either Sherman or me? Especially after everything that had happened.

"Thank you," I finally croaked out. But a bad feeling lingered in my stomach.

I stepped away from Helene and pulled out my cell phone. I dialed Evie's number, but it went straight to voice mail.

"No answer," I said.

A deep frown tugged at Sherman's lips as we moved into the entryway where Helene couldn't hear. "Evie hardly ever turns off her phone."

"I know." I knew she was having a hard time with this, but Evie was anything if not predictable. "I don't know where she would've gone."

But as soon as I said the words, I knew. "She went to the Hanging Hill Highway, didn't she?"

"Why do you think she would go there?" Sherman froze, the only thing moving were his eyes as they flickered with thought.

"Because she wants to see for herself what's going on. I don't know if she's planning on watching the police canines in action or what. My gut feeling is that she wants to check the area out one more time."

Sherman's eyes stilled with concern. "Do you think she's going to go out into the woods herself and look for Angela?"

"I don't know. Let me find out if anyone at the scene has spotted her."

I dialed Daniel's number, and he answered on the second ring. "Hey, Gabby. No updates for you yet, but I assure you we're doing everything we can."

"I'm sure that you are," I said. "But I'm not actually calling about that. Have you, by chance, seen my friend Evie?"

"No, I haven't. Why? Is everything okay?"

My stomach plunged. I'd been hoping he'd say yes, that Evie was there. All my worries could have been dispelled with that one answer. "If you see her, could you just let me know?"

"Will do," he said.

I didn't like this. I didn't like it at all.

Sherman and I took off toward Hanging Hill Highway. I wanted to see if I could put my eyes on Evie myself. After everything that had happened, I didn't want to take any chances. As far as I was concerned, we were all vulnerable.

Sherman was quiet beside me on the drive. I didn't know what he was thinking, but I could only imagine. I knew he cared about Evie deeply. And I knew that, even though Evie didn't want to admit it, she cared deeply about him also.

I had been secretly hoping throughout these months of working on the Cold Case Squad that maybe they would both realize and admit their feelings. But it didn't look like that would be happening. Thank goodness, I didn't have any matchmaker aspirations.

Evie was obviously having a hard time with everything that had happened with Angela. She wasn't handling it as well as I thought she would. I only hoped she hadn't done anything stupid. I knew all about doing stupid things because I had done numerous stupid things for the sake of investigating things myself.

My hands gripped the steering wheel as I headed down the lonely mountain road. Only about five miles from here, Daniel and his crew had set out with the dogs trying to find Angela's scent. It didn't sound like they'd had much luck yet, but I wasn't going to give up hope yet.

Sherman tried Evie's cell phone again, but again it went straight to voice mail.

"I don't like this," Sherman said.

"I don't like it either. I keep hoping we'll find Evie, and she's just sitting at an overlook on the side of the road reflecting on life." Even as those words left my mouth, I knew they were unlikely. But a girl could hope.

As we continued down the fifty-mile stretch of highway, I imagined all those other victims who'd been on this road. I imagined the one who'd broken down. The one who'd hitchhiked. The ones who had stopped at little diners as they had pulled off on side roads into little towns. I imagined the circumstances that had pushed the women to be alone. Had they been trying to find help along the way, only to find tragedy instead?

The thought weighed heavy on my heart. It was an injustice. Those girls deserved better than this. They deserved chances, but those chances had been stripped from them.

The only thing we could do now was to find the person responsible and make sure this person paid. Was that person Big Frankie? Maybe. Cruiser? Could be. Until we knew for sure, I was going to keep looking.

Something about this case had gotten in my blood, and it wouldn't let go of me.

I glanced at my odometer. We only had about fifteen more miles until we reached the end of this highway. There was still no sign of Evie.

I glanced at Sherman out of the corner of my eye and saw the frown on his face. He was worried. Really worried.

Sherman suddenly sat up straighter and pointed to

something on the side of the road. "It looks like our rental. Pull over."

I eased my car onto the side of the road. Wasting no time, Sherman and I hopped out and rushed towards the rental vehicle.

I glanced through the window, but Evie wasn't inside. Just as quickly, I swung my gaze around the area surrounding us, hoping to catch a glimpse of her in the woods.

But she was nowhere to be seen.

Where had our friend gone?

# CHAPTER
# TWENTY-NINE

"EVIE!" I called, my feet snagging on the undergrowth of the forest around me.

Sherman and I had decided to stick together, for safety's sake, as we explored the woods in the area. But, for the past fifteen minutes, we'd been calling for our friend as we searched for her.

Worst-case scenarios tried to play out in my head, but I stopped them. Thinking like that would get me nowhere right now.

We reached a rocky outcropping and paused. I glanced down, noticing the twenty-foot drop into a valley below. I held my breath as I looked down.

I saw nothing but more rocks, trees, and vines.

"I don't know how much farther we should go," I told Sherman. "I think we should call the police—the state police—and see if they can help us. In the meantime, we can look at Evie's car and see if we can find any evidence there."

"I agree that's a good idea. I just don't know where she could've gone."

I had an idea. I didn't want to voice it out loud, though. It sounded too morbid. *But what if the killer wasn't Big Frankie? What if the killer was still out there and had grabbed Evie?*

I tried to set aside the thought and not linger on it too much, but it wouldn't seem to leave my mind. It turned over again and again until a sick feeling remained in my stomach.

We reached my car again, and I pulled out my phone. I didn't have a signal out here. I raised it in the air, like that might help. But it didn't.

"I'm going to have to drive somewhere to find some cell phone service," I told Sherman. "Unless you have more bars than I do?"

He raised his phone also, both of us looking as if we were doing some kind of modern-day ritual to honor an unseen technical dictator. "Not here. But I would like to search her car first."

"Let's look at it quickly, and then we'll go make the phone call. In cases like this . . . well, time usually isn't on our side." I didn't want to say the words, but they were definitely true. *Painfully* true.

Sherman grimaced but nodded. "Okay. Let's check out her car."

I went to the door and, pulling my sleeve over my hand, I opened it. It was unlocked, which was the first sign that not everything was okay. Evie *always* locked her car doors. It was a habit that formed from living in the city.

I was careful not to disturb anything, just in case there was any evidence, as I slid inside. I glanced at the dash. The seats. In the glove box. In crevices.

Everything looked normal and in place. That totally fit neat-and-tidy Evie, but it didn't provide us with any more answers.

"There's nothing here." I couldn't stop the frown that tugged at my lips.

Sherman knelt on the ground and reached under the car. A second later, he sucked in a breath. "Nothing here . . . except this."

He held up her cell phone.

I sucked in a breath. Evie must have dropped it. And the only reason she hadn't picked it up was because something—or someone—had taken her by surprise.

"We've got to call the police," I muttered.

"Yes, we do."

---

I stood near the two state police cars that had arrived at Evie's abandoned car. They were searching the vehicle now for clues they probably wouldn't find. But we needed to go through this process, just in case.

While I waited, I picked up my phone, walked several feet down the road, and finally found a signal. Sherman and I had found it earlier, a magic spot where we were able to make calls. Without moving from that five-inch space, I called Riley to give him an update.

"How are you doing?" He seemed to read between the lines of my words as I tried to put on a brave face in front of the troopers and Sherman.

"I am hanging in. But I'm worried. Every scenario that goes through my mind has a tragic ending."

"I'll be praying that they find Evie. Maybe she just wandered into the woods."

I had a feeling he was just being kind. The likelihood was that she hadn't done that. The likelihood was that the same person behind these other murders had also grabbed her.

Images flashed in my mind, images of finding Evie's body in a field, with bruises at her throat. Where her pale skin had taken on a pasty pallor. Where her eyes were shut—never to open again.

I shivered and pulled my jacket closer. "I'm going to wait around here for a few more hours to see if the police find anything."

"Any updates on Angela?" Riley asked. "You said they sent out dogs to search for her. Any leads?"

I remembered the update Daniel had given me a few

minutes ago. "No, they thought the dogs had picked up on a scent but it was nothing."

I told Riley I loved him and ended the call. Then I turned back to the scene around me. We'd explained to police that Evie wasn't the type to simply go for a walk through the woods. If she had been out here, it had been for a reason. Daniel told me he'd issued a bulletin and that law enforcement was on the lookout for Evie.

"Is there anything around here besides woods?" I asked Daniel as he wrote something on a clipboard near his vehicle. "I've barely seen any houses. Occasionally, I've seen a gravel road leading from the highway. But, *really* . . . what's around here?"

Daniel glanced around and shrugged. "Mostly, this is a hunting area. Up in the hills, there are some cabins. Some of them go back for decades. But from this very spot the nearest restaurant or gas station or business is probably ten or fifteen miles. The nearest town is probably twenty."

"What do people do when their vehicles break down out here? Cell phone service isn't easy to come by. At least, not in my experience."

"We have a safety patrol that monitors these roads. They come by every couple of hours to make sure no motorists are in need of assistance."

"At least there's that." It just seemed so desolate here —not like a place you wanted to experience any issues.

Or a serial killer.

I shivered again.

Another hour passed with no new news. Sherman and I still stood outside in the bitter cold. As the sun set, the temperatures plummeted. But I figured if Evie might be out there in this cold then I should be too. I resisted the temptation to sit in my warm car and wait this out.

But no answers weren't a good thing, and that image of Evie kept flashing in my head.

# CHAPTER
# THIRTY

A NEW HEAVINESS weighed on me as I went back to the bed-and-breakfast that night. I hated to return with no answers, but I didn't know what else I could do. Going out on foot by myself in those woods would do no good. I'd only end up lost and going into hypothermia.

Worse, I'd become another incident that the police needed to investigate. I didn't want to take any resources away from their search for Evie and Angela.

I sat in my room and stared at the profile that Evie had developed for this killer. The fact was, if this killer had grabbed Evie, then this killer was not Big Frankie or Chief Cruiser.

Who did that leave? William Manners? Maybe. Robert Murphy? Probably not.

Unless there was someone I was missing. Certainly

Duncan and Big Frankie had other people who could do their dirty work. The person responsible for these crimes could be somebody who'd been practically invisible during this investigation. Maybe he wasn't even on our radar yet.

I stared at the handwritten notes that I'd taken when Evie had shared her psychological profile of the killer.

She felt like this killer was someone who blended in. Someone who had a grudge against somebody. Somebody who was desperate for control and who had some kind of tragedy in the past that might lead him to do something like this.

I closed my notebook and lifted up a prayer for Evie, for Angela, and for all of the families of the victims out there. There was a serial killer at large, and no one could feel safe knowing that.

A knock sounded at my door. I dragged myself from my notes, stood, and stretched before finally going to answer. I pulled it open, expecting to see Sherman or Helene standing there.

Instead it was . . .

"Riley!" I threw my arms around him. "What are you doing here?"

"It sounded like you could use someone to lean on, so I hopped in my car and I came here."

I pulled away just enough to see his beautiful, intelligent eyes. To stare at his tall, lean frame. To soak in his familiar smile and dark hair. "But what about your case?"

He shrugged. "We don't have court tomorrow, so I took the day off."

I didn't bother to ask how he might be able to do that considering all the pressure of this case. I was just happy that he was here. I reached up and planted a kiss on his lips. I'd missed him.

Riley was here. My Riley.

He was just what I needed right now.

I stepped back and tugged his arm. "Welcome to my humble albeit temporary abode."

"I told the innkeeper that I was your husband and that I wanted to surprise you. She let me come upstairs, but only after checking my driver's license to see if we really had the same last name and address."

I smiled. Helene continued to impress me.

I clung to his hand another moment. "I'm glad she did. And I'm glad you're here. Really glad."

He sat down on the edge of the bed, his gaze turning serious. "Any new updates?"

I sat across from him and ran through everything I knew. When I finished, part of me hoped that he would magically see something I hadn't.

Instead, he squeezed my hand. "Keep digging, Gabby. Keep digging. You'll find answers. I just know that you will."

I overslept and missed breakfast the next morning. Between staying up late and looking for any helpful information online and talking to Riley, I'd hardly gotten any sleep. Besides that, my brain continued to process and re-process everything I knew.

When I'd finally pulled my eyes open, it was nearly lunchtime. I sat up straight in bed, horrified that I'd slept so long. Riley was sitting in the chair in the corner reading. "Morning, sleepyhead."

"You should have woken me."

"I figured you needed your sleep if you were going to think clearly today."

I glanced at my watch and startled before remembering I'd called Margo last night about rescheduling my workshop today. Sherman had told me last night that he'd already rescheduled his flight. Until we knew what was going on with Evie, we weren't leaving here.

I quickly showered and dressed, still scolding myself for oversleeping. When I stepped out of the room, I checked on Sherman. He was on his computer, trying to look up satellite footage, apparently. He told us he'd meet with us in an hour to talk about the day.

In the meantime, Riley and I went downstairs to grab some coffee. Helene poured us cups and Riley and I sat at a breakfast nook, looking outside at the sunny farmland as we sipped our drinks and fueled ourselves with caffeine.

I glanced over at Helene as she cleaned the kitchen, and I could tell she was disturbed over everything that was happening. She barely smiled and her hands trembled as she ran a wet cloth over the butcher block counters.

Finally, she paused and turned toward us. "I'm really sorry to hear about your friend. It seems that none of us are immune to the bad things in life."

"No, I guess, we aren't," I said. "I know you've had your fair share of tough times also."

Giving up her family, walking away from her upbringing, moving to an unwelcoming town, and then losing Tom.

"Yes, I have. I try not to complain, but some days it's harder than others. The Bible says we should rejoice always, pray without ceasing, and give thanks in all circumstances. There are still good people out there. I have to keep reminding myself of that. Take George, for example. He gave up everything to come here and help me out. He didn't have to do that."

"That's great that you have someone like him," I said.

"I suppose, in some ways, our tragedies pulled us together. If he hadn't lost Laurie, and I hadn't lost Tom . . . I guess both of us would have been happier. Of course. But we were able to help each other out. I'm not sure if that makes sense."

"It makes plenty of sense," I said. "We just never know what the future holds, do we?"

"No, we sure don't." She frowned. "George and Tom grew up about an hour north of here. Their lives were so different from mine. Yet we all still had so much in common. We believe in hard work, in appreciating the earth, in respecting others. Sometimes you just have to look for the similarities instead of the differences, you know?"

"The world would be a better place if we did." I smiled and took another sip of my coffee. "Speaking of George, where is he this morning? I want to introduce him to Riley."

Helene began cleaning the countertops again. "Unfortunately, they called him in for an extra shift at work. He wanted to stick around here in case any of Cruiser's men tried to retaliate in any way. But duty calls."

I lowered my cup. "What exactly does George do when he isn't helping out here at your bed-and-breakfast? He said he works for the state."

"He works for the highway safety patrol."

I nodded, surprised by her words. I wasn't sure what I expected her to say, but not that. Then, again, the man seemed pretty capable, so maybe that would be the perfect job for him. "How long has he worked for them?"

"About two years."

Something about her words made me pause.

I remembered Evie's profile.

I mentally shook my head. No, the conclusions I wanted to draw were ridiculous. They weren't grounded in reality. But I couldn't stop thinking about them, thinking about how George fit Evie's profile.

He blended in. Based on the way he ran things on the farm, he liked having a certain measure of control. He had a tragic history. If he worked for the highway safety patrol, he would have the perfect opportunity to find his victims that way.

A sick feeling formed in my gut.

I squeezed my eyes shut.

"What is it Gabby?" Riley studied my face, a knot of concern between his brow.

"It's . . . nothing." I glanced at Helene, unsure if I wanted her to know what I was thinking. Did she have any suspicions about George? Even worse—was she in on this?

I wasn't sure, and I didn't want to take that chance. Quickly, I stood and placed my coffee mug in the sink. "Thank you so much for the coffee, Helene. If you'll excuse me, I need to get upstairs and check on Sherman."

Helene's intelligent eyes studied me. She knew

something was up, but I wasn't ready to tell her what I was thinking. Not yet.

Instead, I took Riley's hand and led him away from the kitchen. I didn't dare speak again until we were in my room with the door shut.

"What's going on, Gabby?" Riley studied me, his eyes narrowed with curiosity.

I turned toward him, my heart racing. "Riley, I know that this might sound crazy, but . . . I wonder if George might be our killer."

His eyes widened. "Why would you say that? I've only heard good things about the man since I've arrived."

I explained my theory to him.

He let out a breath before slowly nodding. "It sounds like it's something worth exploring. But how exactly are you going to do that?"

"I need to get Sherman." I started toward the door. "Maybe he can find something online. If we can find George, maybe we can find Evie also."

I might be way off base here . . . but I didn't think I was.

# CHAPTER
# THIRTY-ONE

I TOLD SHERMAN THE UPDATE. He hadn't discovered anything, but he said my theory sounded plausible. But we had more questions for Helene.

I went downstairs to talk to her, Riley and Sherman following behind.

"Good luck," Riley whispered, squeezing my elbow.

I nodded, needing all the good vibes I could get. Helene was still working in the kitchen when I saw her, and I knew I was going to need to tread very carefully here. If I was right and George was guilty, who was to say Helene wasn't working with him?

I had trouble seeing it. Then again, I had trouble seeing George being involved with this also. He seemed like too nice of a guy. But I needed to explore and know for sure.

"Helene," I called, stopping by the sink where she

washed dishes. Riley and Sherman lingered in the doorway, far enough away not to be imposing but close enough to hear everything that was said. "I know you said George is working, but do you have any idea how we can get in touch with him?"

She looked at me, alarm racing through her eyes. Quickly, she wiped her soapy hands and turned to face me. "Why? Is everything okay?"

"I just need to ask him a couple questions about his girlfriend who went missing two years ago."

"Laurie? Why is that an emergency?"

"Because he asked me to find her. Truth is, I wonder if her disappearance is somehow connected with the other women in this area who have also disappeared."

Helene sucked in a short breath, still wiping her hands. "You really think . . . ?"

"We don't know anything yet, but if I could get some more details from him, that would really help to clear up some things."

"I can try his cell phone." She draped her dishtowel on the side of the sink before picking up her phone and dialing. After several seconds of silence, she ended the call and turned to us. "He didn't answer. I hope everything is okay."

"Maybe he's just helping someone." I kept my voice even. "You said he was a part of the highway safety patrol, right?"

"Yes, that's right. Every Monday and Thursday. He

really loves his job." She picked up a glass tray in front of her. "Cookie?"

"No, thank you." I didn't think I could eat if I wanted to. My stomach was too twisted.

Every Thursday? The victims had been found on Thursdays. Was that because George had been able to leave their bodies while he was on the job?

I pictured it now. Innocent women on the side of the road seeing a member of the highway patrol pull up. Who wouldn't trust someone like that? The pictures that kept forming in my head weren't good.

"What do you know about Hanging Hill Highway?" I asked, leaning against the counter. "Does that have any kind of family connection with Tom, by chance?"

"Hanging Hill Highway?" Helene placed the cookies back onto the kitchen island and squinted her eyes, as if confused. "I don't understand . . ."

"It just goes back to these missing women. I'm wondering if there is any connection there." My throat ached. I didn't want to blow this.

Helene swallowed hard, gripping the kitchen counter. "Hanging Hill Highway is where Laurie disappeared."

I sucked in another quick breath as more pieces fell into place.

"What exactly happened to her again? She went to the store and was never seen again?"

"That's right. There aren't a lot of details to share.

Like I said, she just kind of disappeared off the face of the earth."

"If you don't mind me asking, were she and George engaged or just dating?"

Helene's face looked even paler. "I know that George wanted to propose to her, but I'm not sure that he ever did or that she knew he wanted to. It was such a tragedy. I really liked Laurie a lot."

I licked my lips. "Are there any places along the highway that were special or important to Tom and George?"

She straightened her back and shook her head, something shifting in her gaze. "What's going on here? This is about more than Laurie being missing, isn't it?"

I only had a few seconds to contemplate what to tell her. Should I keep going with my cover story? Or could she handle the truth?

I didn't know. I did know that Helene seemed like a strong woman. She'd impressed me so far. But anyone hearing this news would be shaken.

I exchanged a look with Riley and Sherman. They both nodded at me, giving me confirmation about what I should do.

I stepped toward Helene and prayed I'd find the right words. "Listen, I know how this is going to sound. And this is all just a theory, so please try not to get too upset. But I wonder if George is behind these missing women."

Helene gasped, her hand covering her heart. "Why in the world would you say something like that?"

"Like I said, it's just a theory. We don't know anything for sure. George fits the profile. He has the right job. He has the connection with Hanging Hill Highway."

She shook her head, her eyes squeezing shut. She took a few deep breaths in and then out. When her eyes flung open again, outrage lined her gaze. "I'm going have to ask all of you to leave."

"Helene . . ." I started.

But she turned away. "I mean it. I want you all out. Now."

Riley, Sherman, and I shared a frown. That hadn't gone well. We would get our things, and we would leave. But this was far from being over.

---

Back up in my room, I called Daniel and shared my theory. He agreed that it had merit and promised to help in whatever way he could. But, apparently, dozens of cabins were located along that stretch of highway. There was no way they could search all of them. In my mind, those cabins were our best bet for finding Evie and possibly Angela.

If this killer—possibly George—was guilty, the most logical place he would take a victim would be somewhere private and out of the way, like a hunting cabin. It made the most sense.

I zipped my suitcase, all of my belongings collected. I'd already gone into Evie's room and collected her things, as well. Riley ran them down to his car. I'd figure out what to do with them later. I hoped I would be returning them to her. Soon. I couldn't stomach any other options.

I gave one last glance around my room before heaving my briefcase strap up higher on my shoulder. After walking downstairs, I left a check on the counter for Helene.

She was still busy in the kitchen, this time wiping down all her shelves. Trying to keep herself occupied? Probably.

But I could tell she was still upset, and my heart ached at the sight of her. Her shoulders were hunched, and her eyes looked red as if she'd been crying.

"I'm sorry, Helene." My voice sounded raspy as I paused near her. "I never meant to upset you."

I didn't expect a response. Or, if she did respond, I expected it to be something terse and angry. Instead, she kept cleaning.

After a moment, I stepped away and joined Riley by the back door. Just as I pushed the screen door open, Helene called to me.

I turned toward her and braced myself for whatever she had to say.

She appeared in the kitchen doorway, her normally neat hair falling from its bun and water stains on her apron. But it was the grief on her face that gripped me the most.

"You can search George's place for evidence, if you need to. I'll give you a key." Her voice trembled. "But I'll save you some time. Tom and George's family owns a cabin off of old State Route 123—it's right off Hanging Hill Highway. They have about twenty-five acres there."

My heart raced. That was exactly what I needed to know. "Thank you."

She nodded, but more tears welled in her eyes. "I don't want him to be guilty."

"I don't want him to be either," I told her quietly.

We left Riley's car at the bed-and-breakfast and climbed into mine. We had to head out to that area and see what we could find out.

I glanced at my watch. It was already three. We were burning daylight.

# CHAPTER
# THIRTY-TWO

I HARDLY KNEW what to say as we drove along the mountain road. A gloomy gray surrounded us, giving an overall eerie feeling to the entire area.

The trees, once cheerful with the bloom of fresh leaves, now looked skeletal and imposing. To make matters worse, it was hard to see the road in front of us as fog had begun to settle into the deep crevices between the mountains.

Riley drove my car, and I sat in the front seat beside him, trying to act as navigator.

"You really think she's going to be here?" Sherman asked.

I glanced back at him. "I have no idea. But this is our best lead. It only makes sense, if George is guilty, that he has somewhere private he's taking his victims."

"Why Evie?" Sherman asked.

I'd asked myself that also. "My guess is that George found her on the side of the road. When Evie saw him pull up and realized what his job was . . . maybe George got scared. He feared she would realize the truth and wanted to keep her quiet."

"I just don't understand." Sherman shook his head, his voice dull with worry. "He seemed like such a nice guy."

"A lot of killers have seemed like nice guys. It's hard to know what's going on behind the façade that people put forward," Riley said. "My friend is working on a case right now where a woman killed her best friend. On the outside, the two of them looked as tight as tight could be. But, apparently, this woman had resented her friend for years, and all that emotion came out in a moment of rage. Just goes to prove you can't judge a person's criminal intent based only on their looks."

"I suppose, on a logical level, I know that," Sherman said. "But I only get to see these things behind the scenes usually. It still freaks me out to see evil face-to-face like this."

I shivered at his words. Whoever was behind this *was* evil. And delusional. And all kinds of messed up in so many different ways.

The only thing I could figure was that something had happened with George's girlfriend that set him off in this direction. I wasn't justifying it, nor could I imagine what it might've been. But somehow that event changed the trajectory of his future.

"Are we getting close?" Riley scanned the road ahead.

I glanced at my GPS. Despite the remote location, it was still working, though I couldn't see many road names. "According to the information from Helene, the road leading to their property should be right up there on the left."

The knot in my stomach tightened and grew larger by the moment. I wondered if Daniel was there yet and if he had discovered anything.

"Right here." I pointed to a gravel road that looked even more off-grid than the road we were currently on. Not only that, but it snaked upward, higher into the hills.

Riley turned, and we climbed up the road less traveled. The fog seemed heavier here, as did the danger. Not only were we potentially getting closer to a killer, but this road, even on a bright, sunshiny day, would seem treacherous.

I gripped the armrest beside me and kept my eyes glued in front of me. I didn't know how close we were to the actual cabin itself, but I knew we needed to be careful not to alert anyone to our presence. The gravel road would make that more difficult.

Finally, the woods cleared in front of us. Was this it? Were we finally here?

As we turned the corner, three police cars came into view.

This was it, I realized. This was the property that we'd been looking for.

My heart pounded as I anticipated what we might find inside.

---

Riley pulled to the side and cut his lights. Quietly, we stepped out of the car and walked toward the state police cruisers parked there. A moment later, Daniel spotted us.

"My guys are searching inside right now," Daniel said.

"Anything?" I held my breath until I heard his answer.

"So far, no. But there is evidence that someone has recently been here. There's fresh trash, a few footprints, some droplets of water in the sink."

Did that mean that George had been here with one of his victims? But where was he now?

"I did a quick search on this Laurie woman on the way here," Daniel said. "Turns out, her disappearance does match the same pattern as our other victims. The only difference is that her body has never shown up. I am going to do some more research and maybe talk to some of her friends to see if I can get a better read on the situation between her and George."

I prayed that my gut instinct was correct, and George was the one behind this. Otherwise, I was wasting time and resources. I didn't want that to happen. Not when time was of the essence.

Riley reached down and laced his fingers with mine, almost as if he could sense my rising anxiety. Meanwhile, I glanced at Sherman. I'd never seen his face look so tense and withdrawn.

He never even had the chance to tell Evie how he felt. Or maybe he *had* had the chance, but he hadn't taken it, which might even make him feel worse. Lost opportunities were always hard to swallow.

A few minutes later, a trooper strode back toward Daniel. "There's no one inside. But, like we said earlier, there is evidence that someone has been here recently."

"Any indications as to whom that might've been?" Daniel asked.

"There was a footprint. Based on the size of it, I would say it was a woman."

"And that's it?" Daniel stared at his trooper.

The man nodded. "That's it."

Daniel let out a long sigh and stared off into the distance. I could see his thoughts churning. Finally, he sighed again and turned back to me.

"I'm not sure there's anything here, Gabby," he said.

My heart pounded in my ears. This wasn't what I wanted to hear.

"I think you have good instincts, but we have no evidence that this George guy is guilty. I looked into his background, and it's squeaky clean. Not even a parking ticket. He has no history of violence. Nothing."

"I know, but there's evidence he's been here."

"And there's no crime in that. This is his place. He can come and go as he pleases."

I opened my mouth, wanting to argue more. But I knew it would be useless. Instead, I asked, "So you're leaving?"

"There's nothing else we can do here. I'm sorry."

I knew his words were true. He was going to need more to go on before he put further resources and time into it. I couldn't blame him. But that didn't stop the disappointment from coming.

He tapped the side of my arm as if giving me an A for my efforts.

But as the police cruisers pulled away, my heart sunk. This had been my best lead. If George and Evie weren't here, then where in the world might they have gone? I had no other ideas.

Riley, Sherman, and I stood there in silence after the police left. Darkness had fallen, and it almost felt heavy and imposing as it closed in on us. But, for the moment, I hardly cared.

"What now?" Sherman placed his hands on his hips, his lips pulling down in disappointment also.

"I'm all out of ideas," I said. "Anybody else have any?"

No one said anything for a minute.

"We just can't give up," Sherman finally said, his voice cracking.

"I'm not ready to give up either, but I don't know what else we can do. For all we know, Helene may have tipped George off. Maybe he was here, but he left." I didn't like the thought of it, but I had to acknowledge it was a possibility.

"Since we're here, why don't we go take a look at that cabin ourselves," Riley suggested, nodding toward the building in the distance. "The police don't seem to think it's a crime scene, so we shouldn't be disturbing anything."

I nodded, impressed with his idea. "Maybe there will be some kind of other clue there."

Pulling up the flashlight app on our phones, we made our way to the rustic log cabin that sat in the clearing in front of us. When I said rustic, I meant rustic. This was not a vacation rental. This place probably ran on a generator and was heated with a fireplace. I doubted there would be any electricity available inside.

Riley helped me up the rickety wooden steps leading to the front door. My throat clogged with a moment of fear. I'd been in a lot of bad situations before. My only comfort was knowing that Daniel and his men had just been in here. The place should be clear.

We stepped inside and shined our lights around. Like I suspected, the place was nothing fancy. There was a worn couch, end tables, and an outdated dinette in the corner. The kitchen cabinets looked at least four decades old, and the countertop was yellow with age. Several stuffed deer heads stared at us from above a small fireplace.

Sherman found a kerosene lantern and lit it. As light filled the room, I slid my phone back into my pocket.

It couldn't hurt to give the place a good look. I wanted to know who might have been here.

I walked to the trashcan and saw that some canned beans had been opened and discarded. I picked up one can and noted that the leftovers were still moist. If these were old, any residue would be dry by now. I hoped Daniel and his guys had taken some of these for evidence.

My heart lifted for a moment. Despite Daniel's initial evaluation, I still thought we might be onto something.

I paced toward the sink and saw a fork there. Someone had definitely been staying here. Hiding here. Even the old blanket that had been left strewn on the couch seemed to indicate that.

Just what happened here in this cabin? Did I even want to know?

"Hey guys," Sherman said. "Over here."

I walked across the cabin. Sherman had pulled something off of the bookshelf. I leaned in for a closer look. It was a photo of five men holding hunting rifles and wearing camo. George appeared to be the second man on the left. Woods stretched behind them, along with a small cabin.

I wasn't sure what was significant about the photo.

"What if this picture was taken here on this property?" Sherman asked.

I squinted. "It doesn't look like the cabin. It looks too small, and there are too many trees around it."

"Exactly." Sherman's eyes lit. "Helene said they had twenty-five acres here. I know some guys back in Kansas who have properties like this. Some of them have more than one cabin on their land. They bring groups of guys up here to go hunting together."

I let his words sink in. "So you think there's another building around here? Somewhere else where George could be hiding?"

"I think it's a possibility worth exploring."

So did I. Then again, right now, I thought every idea was worth exploring.

# CHAPTER
# THIRTY-THREE

RILEY, Sherman, and I spent the next thirty minutes looking through everything else at the cabin. Finally, in the bottom of a drawer in the bedroom, Sherman found an old land survey.

The document had probably come with the land when the family purchased it. And, based on some marks on the paper, there was another cabin about three miles from this one.

"It looks like there might be a small lane that leads to it." Riley pointed to a line on the paper. "Maybe that's a trail and hunters have to hike into the area. It's not all that uncommon."

"So how are we going to get there? I'm not crazy about the idea of hiking three miles in the dark." And, I had to admit, it was cold outside—probably thirty-some degrees with a brisk wind. I hadn't brought a heavy coat or even a hat with me. That wasn't to say that I wouldn't venture out there for Evie. I just needed to know that it was the best way to proceed.

"I think we should try to drive to the area first," Riley said. "It just makes more sense. If someone is there, we're going to need a vehicle to get away."

I nodded, relieved at his suggestion. It made perfect sense. "Let's go see what we can find out."

We climbed back into the car and headed along the path marked on the map. My sedan wasn't made to go off-roading, and I hoped it held up okay. Then again, I'd rather the car be damaged than the people inside. Sherman held the land survey in his hands and tried to follow along as we went.

"It looks like we need to pull into the woods over there." He pointed to a small opening in the distance.

I squinted, trying to imagine our car fitting into that area. I wasn't sure it was going to happen. But we wouldn't know until we got a little closer.

Finally, we reached the fog-entrenched opening. It was going to be tight, but we might be able to squeeze through. No doubt, my car would contain a few more scratches at the end of this, but I was okay with that.

That didn't stop my heart from pounding furiously against my chest as we continued forward. It was nearly impossible to see anything except the road in front of us. I had no idea if there were cliffs or streams or any other kinds of dangers just waiting for us out of sight.

That was why I had to just keep focusing on the road ahead.

"How much farther?" Riley's hands were white-knuckled on the steering wheel.

"It's hard to say," Sherman said. "But based on my calculations, we've only gone about two miles."

These were two of the longest miles of my life. Two miles in the city went by quickly. But two miles on a back road in the mountains at night might as well be two hours.

We kept moving forward, the car bouncing against the rocks beneath us. Branches scraped against the car, an ominous warning of what we were doing.

I suppose it would've been a good idea to let Daniel know that we'd discovered this. But I didn't want to call him out for another false alarm. I could feel that I was already treading on thin ice, and I'd used one too many favors with him.

With every second that passed, Evie's chances of survival grew slimmer and slimmer. I couldn't stand the thought of something happening to my friend. I squeezed my eyes shut at the idea.

No, I couldn't think like that. I had to think only good thoughts here.

A half mile from the site, the road ended. Riley put the car in park and turned to us. "What now?"

I stared ahead to where a trail opened up. "It looks like we have to go the rest of the way on foot."

"Are you sure you want to do that?" Riley asked. "We don't know what's out there, and there's not going to be anyone to help us if we get in trouble."

"What other choice do we have?" I asked.

"I'll support whatever you decide," Riley said.

That was just another reason I loved him. We'd come a long way in the years we'd been together.

"We've come this far. I can't turn back now."

Riley nodded and reached for the door handle. "That's what I thought you would say. Come on. Let's go."

We climbed out, and another shiver raked through me. There was just something about the woods at night that could creep me out. I hoped we were doing the right thing. I only knew that I couldn't live with myself unless I did everything I could to find some answers.

Riley led the way, gripping my hand as we walked the narrow path through the woods. Sherman brought up the rear. The forest was eerily quiet around us, as if the residents here knew about our escapade. Or was their silence a way of warning us that we shouldn't be here?

I didn't know. I just continued forward, one foot in front of the other.

Finally, the woods cleared. There in front of us was the cabin we'd been looking for.

And a faint light shone in the window.

This had to be it. I started to take off toward the cabin when I felt a hand on my shoulder. Riley.

"We can't just rush in there. If George is there, he probably has a gun."

"He's right," Sherman whispered. "I've been trying to get a phone signal out here, but I don't have one. We're on our own."

"We've got to make sure this isn't another wild goose chase," I said. "We need to look inside that building, but we don't have any time to waste."

"What should we do?" Sherman asked.

I chewed on it for only a few seconds before coming up with a plan. "Sherman, why don't you drive until you get a signal and tell Daniel exactly what's going on here? In the meantime, Riley and I will stay here and figure out something to do."

"I don't want you to get yourselves killed." He pushed his glasses up again, worry staining his gaze.

"I don't want us to get ourselves killed either. That's why I remembered to bring some protection this time." I reached into my waistband and pulled out my Glock. Thank goodness for states having reciprocal concealed carry laws.

"I still don't like this," Sherman said.

"No one does, and I won't use it unless I have to. But if Evie's in there we don't have time to waste."

Finally, he nodded. "Be safe."

Riley handed him the keys and he hurried back toward the car. When he was gone, I turned to Riley, and our gazes met. I felt the tension between us— tension not because we were upset with each other, but tension because we both understood the implications of this situation.

I licked my lips. "What do you want to do?"

"I think we should peek in the windows to see who's inside. But we don't make any sudden moves without talking to each other, deal?"

"Yes, deal."

Moving swiftly, we hurried across the grass toward the cabin. The windows were just high enough that I couldn't see inside. But a voice drifted out.

*George's* voice drifted out.

My heart pounded harder. We were in the right place. Now I just needed Sherman to get back here with Daniel and a whole swarm of state troopers.

Using his hands like a stirrup, Riley boosted me, and I peeked in the window. I sucked in a breath at what I saw. Evie sat in a chair, her arms bound behind her. Angela was beside her, also tied up.

I scanned the rest of the space. The cabin looked like it had been trashed or like a fight had happened. Tables were knocked over, papers were scattered, dishes were strewn.

My gaze went back to Evie and Angela. A bruise

colored the skin around Angela's eye, and her lip appeared busted.

My heart thudded into my chest. What exactly had gone on here?

George paced in front of them. His hair looked wild and his eyes crazy.

He'd had some kind of mental breakdown, hadn't he? Something had snapped in him. Or maybe this side of his personality had just been lying dormant until he found his next opportunity.

Whatever it was, he wasn't playing any games.

He stopped in front of Evie and leered at her. "I just need you to tell me that you love me."

"You need help," Evie said, her lips barely moving. "How many times do I have to tell you that?"

"You're exactly like my girlfriend. She wasn't the type to capitulate, even when her life was on the line." He scowled. "Tell me you love me!"

"No." Evie raised her chin.

"Tell me!" George demanded, getting in her face and gripping her arms. "Don't you know how much I love you? I only want to take care of you."

"George, this isn't the way we need to do things," Angela said. "There are better ways."

George's gaze flung toward Angela. "You're not even supposed to be here."

"But I am here. And I'm glad I am. You can't hurt my daughter. Please, let her go."

When I saw a tear escape down Evie's cheek, a small sob escaped from my lips.

Riley lowered me back to the ground. "What is it? Are you okay?"

I swallowed back my emotions, trying to stay focused on solutions instead of my fear. "It looks like George is losing it. I don't know how much more time they have, Riley."

Before we could formulate our next step, a new sound cut through the air. My gaze jerked toward the front of the cabin, but I couldn't see anything.

As if reading my mind, Riley boosted me back up to the window. When he did, I saw Sherman burst inside and tackle George.

# CHAPTER
## THIRTY-FOUR

I TURNED TO RILEY. "We've got to get in there. Now."

We rushed toward the front door. We barged inside just as George slammed his fist into Sherman's jaw. Sherman recoiled, grasping his face.

"Sherman!" Evie screamed.

George swung again, this time punching Sherman in his gut. Sherman let out an *oof* before falling to the floor. His face scrunched with pain.

George's gaze jerked toward us, something primal emerging in his dilated eyes. His head jerked toward something on the floor.

His gun, I realized as I followed his stare.

We lunged toward it at the same time. My foot hit it first. The shotgun slid across the wood floor out of reach.

For now.

Riley grabbed George and shoved him against the wall. Flipping him over, Riley grabbed his arms and clutched them at his back. The motion effectively trapped George, not allowing him to move.

"You've got this all wrong," George muttered. "Let me go."

"I'll let the police decide what to do with you," Riley muttered.

All my husband's martial arts training was paying off. Thank goodness.

Heaving in a deep breath, I looked at Sherman. He pulled himself up from the floor but still held his jaw.

"You okay?"

He nodded, even as his eyes squinted with discomfort. "I'll be fine."

With that assurance, I rushed toward Evie and began to work the ropes around her wrists.

"Boy, am I glad to see you." Evie's voice cracked, and another tear washed down her cheek. Her makeup was long gone, her hair tousled, and her clothes dirty. But I didn't see any major injuries.

"Are you hurt?" I asked, my fingers trying to untangle the knot.

"No. Nothing that won't heal, at least."

I pulled another loop, and the rope fell from her wrists. She flung herself from her seat and threw her arms around Angela. A sob escaped as she buried her face against her mom. "I'm so glad you're okay. I thought you might be dead and I'd never see you again."

Angela nodded, tears filling her eyes also. "I'm so glad you're okay too, Evie."

Evie pulled back and glanced at Sherman. I could see the war going on inside her, and I moved toward Angela. "Let me untie her."

"Thanks." She looked at Angela. "Give me a minute."

Evie rushed across the room and knelt beside Sherman. Tenderly, she touched his face where George had punched him. Maybe this near-death experience had softened her heart some.

I hoped.

"Oh, Sherman," she whispered. "I never thought I would see you do something like that. You were so brave."

Sherman's face glowed, despite his injury. He reached for her, wiping her hair from her eyes. "I love you, Evie. I always have, and I always will. I couldn't stand the thought of something happening to you."

"I thought you were never going to tell me that," she whispered. Evie kissed his forehead before cradling him in her arms.

Riley and I exchanged a look. That was the last thing I had expected to see. But nothing made me happier.

I turned toward Angela and worked to untie her.

Her face was dirty, her hair matted, and her clothes stained.

Whatever had happened here, it hadn't been good.

"Are we ever glad to see you," I said.

"I'm glad to see you guys too." She offered a sad smile. "But I never meant to get you all involved with this."

"I knew Evie would never sleep at night unless she had answers. But I still don't understand how you ended up here." I got one knot loose but still had another to work on.

"I stumbled upon the cabin. He caught me and chained me to the floor. The girl I'd followed was already dead." A sob escaped, and her body trembled with grief. "I was too late."

Finally, the knot released and I pulled the rope from around her. Angela stood, shaking out her hands. As she took a step forward, she wobbled. She'd been injured, I realized. No wonder she hadn't been able to run.

There would be time to hear the rest of the story later. For now, I glanced around the space. Angela joined Evie and Sherman on the floor. Riley still held George, who muttered beneath his breath.

I was just glad everyone was okay.

Because this could have turned out so differently. So, so differently.

The sun began to rise, and we were all still at George's little cabin in the woods. The state police were here, collecting evidence. They had taken George into custody. Paramedics had also shown up, and they were checking out Evie, Angela, and Sherman. They all appeared to be okay, though Angela was dehydrated and needed fluids.

I felt slightly dazed as I watched everything unfold in front of me. I still couldn't believe this was finally over. I hadn't had the chance to talk to anyone during the flurry of activity, and I still craved more answers.

Finally, when I saw the paramedics walk away from the ambulance, I approached Evie, Sherman, and Angela.

"Thanks for looking for me." Evie's chin trembled as she said the words. "When I first started this case, I thought that everybody I ever cared about was destined to let me down. But all of you have proved me wrong, and I can't tell you how grateful I am for that."

Sherman moved to sit beside her, and she reached for his hand. The two of them exchanged a smile.

"You know I'll always be there for you," he murmured, holding an ice pack to his jaw.

She nodded and rubbed beneath her eye, as if struggling to hold back her emotions.

I wanted to tell her we'd always be stronger together.

But I didn't have to say the words aloud. I suspected she already knew.

"If you don't mind me asking, what happened?" I asked her. "We found your car but . . ."

"I was stupid, I suppose." Evie frowned. "I mean, I should have known better. I've been around the block a few times too. But I couldn't stop thinking about Angela being out here in the woods by herself. I was going stir-crazy just sitting in the house and not doing anything, so I drove out to this road. I didn't expect to find anything. I just wanted to visit the area again. It's like my heart was calling me back."

I remained quiet, giving her the space she needed to talk and to formulate her thoughts.

"I pulled over on the side of Hanging Hill Highway and climbed out. I stood there, looking at the little stream as it babbled past and trying to figure out if I could possibly leave this place without having any answers. I realized that I couldn't, but that I needed to trust the process I had put so much of my time and faith into. I am a part of the process, and if I can't say that I trust it, then why am I even doing this job?"

She had a good point. I had to come to those realizations in my own life more than once. Riley joined us, slipping his arm around my waist as we listened.

"Someone pulled up behind me. A safety patrol officer." Evie's voice cracked. "I figured he'd pulled over to see if I had broken down. Imagine my surprise when I saw George step out. At first, I was happy to see him. But, then, I noticed a strange look in his eyes. I tried to get in my car and get away. I knew something bad was about to happen. But, before I could, he tased me. I was immobile. He put me in the trunk of his car, and he drove me up here."

"That's when we were reunited." Angela offered a sad smile. She rubbed her wrists still, and her lips looked dry and chapped.

My gaze remained on her. I was anxious to hear her side of the story as well. "Would you mind starting at the beginning?"

I'd put some of the pieces together in my mind, but I was anxious to know if I was correct or not.

"I came to Shady Valley for more than one reason," she started. "I'd met that man online, and I figured Evie wouldn't approve of him. Or that no one would, for that matter. That's why I kept it to myself. I'd just learned that my big brother lived in Shady Valley. I was able to find a grainy picture of him that was about fifteen years old."

"We found that on the ground not too far from where your car had been left," I told her.

She drew in a shaky breath, obviously still reeling over the night's events. "While I was waiting for my date at the restaurant, I saw a girl crying. I talked to her and sensed something was wrong. She told me she'd run away from home and didn't know what she was going to do. I offered to drive her somewhere, but she refused and left the restaurant."

I waited for her to continue.

"For a moment, I wondered if I should just let her go," Angela said. "But then I realized I couldn't. When I went outside to try to catch her, she was gone. I rushed down the sidewalk, asking people if they had seen her. No one had."

"That's when you ran into William Manners," I said.

Angela nodded. "I did. Halfway through our conversation, I realized who he was. I didn't have time to explain—I didn't have a minute to waste. I needed to find this girl before I worried about that. I told myself I would come back and find him again later. I kept searching, and finally I ran into someone who told me he'd seen this girl walking toward Hanging Hill Highway."

"What happened next?" I asked.

"I got in my car and took off after her. I was hoping to catch her and convince her to let me help her in some way. I know the statistics. I know that the future for someone in her position isn't good. It would either end in human trafficking, prostitution, or drug use. I didn't want to see any of those things happen to her."

"So how did your car end up in the woods?" Riley asked.

"I saw her get into a car with somebody." Angela grimaced and rubbed her brow. "A safety patrol vehicle.

I was a good distance behind them. But when I saw the car pull off onto a back road, I became suspicious. I followed behind, but I knew it would be too conspicuous to keep going up those roads behind them. So I pulled into the brush and covered up my car. I decided I'd try to go the rest of the way on foot."

"What happened then?" I asked.

She looked down at her lap as if embarrassed. "I got discombobulated in the woods. I couldn't find my way back to the car or to the road. So I kept walking. I was hungry and thirsty and tired, but the last straw came when I stepped on a rock and twisted my ankle. I was in the middle of nowhere, and I could hardly walk."

I blanched as I thought about the predicament she'd been in.

These past few weeks had to have been grueling for her.

"I managed to get myself to a clearing, and I saw a cabin. I didn't have a cell phone, so I couldn't call for help. I hoped if I stayed long enough maybe somebody would come. Eventually, they did. But it was George. He found me. He tased me and brought me to the other cabin, this more secluded one. The girl from the restaurant was there but she was . . . dead." Angela wiped the tears from beneath her eyes.

"It's okay if you don't want to finish," I told her.

"No, I need to finish." Angela drew in a deep breath.

"He chained my ankle to a stove and left me food and water. He'd come by to check on me periodically."

"And then he showed up with Evie . . ." I muttered. I could hardly breathe as I waited to hear the rest of the story.

"That's right. I couldn't believe it." Angela wiped away another tear.

"And I can fill in some more of the story from here," Daniel said joining us. "I've been looking into George's background. It turns out his girlfriend told her friends that George had violent tendencies and was possessive. She tried to get away, to escape the relationship, but he must have followed her. We're working on a location of her car and her body, but we believe that George killed her and that was when his psychotic break started."

A chill swept over me. Though I wasn't surprised, this wasn't exactly the ending that I wanted.

"Thank you all for taking care of my Evie for me." Angela grabbed her daughter's hand and squeezed it. The two of them exchanged a look.

I was so happy to see their reunion. Nothing made my heart feel better.

A few minutes later, it was decided that Sherman would ride with Evie to the hospital. Daniel had insisted that they all needed to be checked out more anyway. That meant Riley and I were free to go .

As we walked back toward my car, Riley took my hand.

"What do you think will happen with Helene?" I asked.

"My guess is that she'll move. She can't manage that property on her own, and maybe this will help solidify that realization for her. I have a feeling she was living out her husband's dreams anyway. Maybe it would be best for her to move."

"And the town? Do you think anything will change?"

Riley shrugged. "Everyone there is related. But the mayor will have some pressure on him now. I personally think William Manners would make a great police chief."

"I think that's a wonderful idea. I can't wait for him and Angela to be reunited. Maybe we will have some happy endings here."

"Maybe we will." Riley stopped me. He reached into his pocket and pulled something out. "Gabby Thomas, will you marry me all over again?"

I looked down and saw . . . "It's my ring! You got it back."

"I did. I was just trying to find the right time to tell you." He grinned and slipped it onto my finger.

The gold band had never looked better. "I can't tell you how glad I am to have it back. You did disinfect it, right?"

He chuckled. "I did. And I'm pretty glad that you have it back also. Speaking of which, I'm supposed to pass on a message to you that your dad and Teddi have finally set a wedding date."

I sucked in a quick breath. "Really? I can't believe it. This whole time I thought they were just joking with us or something."

"No joke. They both seem very excited. They'll be getting married in two months."

"It sounds like we have a lot of changes ahead."

"It sure does, doesn't it? But I know that as long as you and I have each other—and God—everything will be okay."

I squeezed his hand back. "You're absolutely right."

I reached up on my tiptoes and planted a kiss on his lips. It didn't matter that we both looked terrible and had been awake all night. There was no one else I would rather do life with than Riley Thomas. From now until forever.

~~~

Thank you so much for reading *Clean Break*. If you enjoyed this book, please consider leaving a review!

Keep reading for a preview of *Cleans to an End*.

# AVAILABLE NOW

# CLEANS TO AN END: CHAPTER ONE

"So, Carson hasn't called me back since we went out. Why do I always date the wrong guy, Gabby? Am I cursed? Stupid? Too pretty for my own good?" Clarice Wilkinson paused from scrubbing the floor and looked at me through her hazmat goggles as if I held all the answers.

I *should* hold these kinds of answers. I'd dated every kind of wrong guy before I finally married Riley. I was *so* glad I wasn't in the dating world anymore. So. So. Glad. Like, I'd rather swim through crime-scene sludge than try to find Mr. Right again.

"Listen, this guy is showing his true character," I told her. "That's a good thing. Be glad he's out of your life now instead of after you've invested more in the relationship."

I wiped up some more dried blood from the golden

oak floor of a top-grain house in Norfolk, Virginia. The place was a study in contrasts. Peaceful yellow walls. Freshly waxed floors. And a pool of blood and the subsequent spatter around it.

"My clock is ticking." Clarice's eyes narrowed with over-strung drama. "I want to settle down and have kids."

If she worked as much as she talked, we'd be done with this job a lot faster. But I had a feeling she needed a listening ear, and here I was . . . I might as well use all my bad experiences for good. That's what Jean Valjean from *Les Mis* would have told me to do.

"You're only twenty-three, right?"

"Exactly." Her eyes widened, driving home her point. "I'm getting old. I had all these prospects in college, yet all I wanted was to play the field. Now that I've graduated? All the good ones are gone."

"I'm sorry to hear that?" My voice trailed off into a question.

"You're so lucky you met Riley." Clarice pushed her goggles farther up onto her face and began scrubbing more dried blood from the floor. "When am I going to meet *my* Riley?"

I wished I could answer that for her. But I couldn't. Besides, in my book, Riley was one of a kind.

"Okay, enough about that depressing subject. Do you remember when we first started working together?" Clarice changed topics like Katy Perry changing outfits during a concert. "You used to always play with different jingles. That was so much fun. Let's do it again."

I hadn't tried to come up with a jingle in a long time. But at one point in my life, I'd prided myself in my ability to manipulate lyrics into silly little crime-scene ditties.

"There was one I always thought you should use." Clarice rocked back on her knees—in other words, she stopped working again. "How did it go?"

I shrugged, not sure which one she was referring to. I'd come up with quite a few. Some sounded more like cheers. Some were to the tune of nursery rhymes. I even tried rap a few times and tapped into my Gabby G-Dog persona.

Before I could offer any suggestions, she started singing one of my "Santa Claus Is Coming to Town" remakes. "If you've been shot, if you've been stabbed, if blood on your walls say 'Someone's been bad,' Trauma Care is the-e-re for you."

Wow. It had been a long time since I'd thought about that little song I'd written. "You've got a great memory."

"It would have been a fantastic jingle." She began scrubbing again. "I can totally hear Zooey Deschanel singing it, kind of like she did on *Elf*."

I tried not to snort. "Of course, Trauma Care is no longer the name of the business."

I'd sold my part of the company to Chad Davis,

who'd eventually rebranded. He was now Squeaky Clean Restoration Services.

Clarice shook her head, as if put off by the name change. "So boring. Maybe we can make a jingle for him. Maybe to the tune of 'Twinkle, Twinkle Little Star'? Squeaky Clean is the best. All the others don't pass the test. Cleaning blood is what we do. You should just hope it's not you. Squeaky Clean is the best. And we do our job with zest."

She used jazz hands to pull the whole song together. That, when combined with her hazmat suit, made for a real winner.

"I'm sensing a second career in your future," I told her, not bothering to keep the smile out of my tone.

"I'm sensing sarcasm." Clarice looked up for long enough to shoot me a playful frown. "Let's get back to those jingles a little later. What's going on with you lately?"

I'd forgotten how much my prissy sidekick liked to talk. My prissy *former* sidekick. It *had* been a while since the two of us had caught up.

At times when we were cleaning, it felt like it had been *ages* since I'd done something like this. At other times, I felt like I'd never stopped cleaning up blood, brain matter, and other gruesome aftermaths of death.

I used a scrub brush to get a particularly stubborn bloodstain from the floorboard, glad for my protective equipment. "Grayson Technologies was sold out to a larger company, and they're still restructuring, which basically means they want to keep me close but not too close."

"I see."

"Besides, with everything going on right now, forensic trainings are on hold. Instead of learning how to properly apply fingerprint dust, now all the police departments want to learn about is proper law enforcement etiquette. That's what they're calling it. Etiquette."

"You should write a paper on it. It can be called 'Law Enforcement Etiquette in a Time of Cultural Wokeness and Perpetual Offense.'"

"That title alone would offend people."

"And further drive home your point. Or you could write a song. It could be 'A Soliloquy on Proper Behavior for Crime Fighting in the Key of E Minor.'"

I forgot how funny Clarice could be. She was an entertaining gal. Maybe even a bit like me when I was younger.

Clarice pushed her dirty rags across the floor as we scoured every inch of the room. "Anyway, that's crazy about your job. Things can change in a flash, can't they?"

"Yes, they can." For instance, I never saw myself in this line of work again, not after I'd progressed to bigger and better things. But that was neither here nor there.

"What about your cold cases? I thought that dreamy Garrett Mercer had you busy with that." As she said

Garrett's name, her voice became wispy and her eyes cloudy.

Garrett had that effect on women.

"He does," I told her. "But now that Evie and Sherman are married, they requested a month off. Who am I to deny them the honeymoon of their dreams?"

"Where did they go?"

"New Zealand so they could see Middle Earth."

"Middle Earth?" Clarice glanced at me in confusion. "Is that a band?"

"A band? No."

"An amusement park?"

"What? No. It's a—"

"I know! An archeological expedition!"

"Clarice, Middle Earth is from Tolkien."

She stared at me. "Oh, he's that designer, right? I know someone who has a cute purse like that she bought on eBay . . ."

I resisted the urge to palm my forehead. "Haven't you ever heard of *Lord of the Rings*?"

She twisted her neck as if thinking a little too hard about her answer. "I've heard of that somewhere. It's a movie with those little hobbit people, right? Sounds weird to me."

I shook my head, not even trying to understand her thought process. "What's weird to one person is perfect for someone else."

"Well, while those two are out pretending to be

incredibly short creatures searching for a designer hand-bag, I'm glad you're here with me. Their loss is my gain."

If she wasn't entertaining me so much with her ditzi-ness, I might roll my eyes.

She continued to chatter. "But I'm really sorry that Tommy broke his leg."

Tommy, one of Chad's employees, had fallen from a ladder, and now he was off his feet for at least two months.

It worked out well for me because I was able to fill in and make some cash in the meantime.

Not that Riley and I were hurting for money. Riley was a lawyer, and he was doing fine at his new practice. But I'd never been one to sit at home doing nothing. Besides, it felt good to get back to my roots.

"So what happened here?" Clarice continued, frowning at all the blood we still had left to remove.

"From what I understand, an intruder broke into this woman's home, shot her, and then stole all her money and jewelry."

"I didn't think people did that anymore," Clarice said. "Isn't it so much easier to rip off people's identities or steal their credit card numbers online?"

I wanted to argue, but I couldn't. Her words were so true. "For real. You'd think criminals would know better, right? Now a life has been needlessly lost. All for a measly few hundred dollars."

"I hate to imagine how things played out here."

"I can imagine it a little too well," I told her.

Based on blood evidence, the victim had been standing in the sunroom when the intruder had stepped behind her, taking her by surprise.

He'd shot her once, based on the bullet hole in the wall.

Blood impact from the wound had spattered on the wall.

The victim had fallen to the floor and bled out. Her body had remained there until her family found her the next morning.

The killer had run in the opposite direction, careful not to leave any footprints in the aftermath of the crime.

As always, the crime scene told the story.

One had to just be willing to listen.

Clarice moved to the other side of the sunroom, where the crime had occurred.

This wasn't just any sunroom. It was an exquisite second-story sunroom in a lovely neighborhood.

Windows surrounded us and were filled with leafy green plants that hung and stood and floated, reminding me of a 1950s housewife edition of *Avatar*. A leather couch sat against the wall, and wicker furniture formed a conversation area around it. Not my style, but the place was peaceful and serene.

If it wasn't for the blood.

Clarice and I still had a lot of work to do. Not only

did we have to sanitize this place, but we also needed to check the furniture and the walls for any particulates that we may have missed.

The woman's son had hired us for the job. He couldn't face this himself. Most people whose loved one had been through crimes like this couldn't.

I didn't blame them.

I'd started doing this work after I'd had to drop out of college. I'd always wanted to be involved with crime-scene investigation. When I couldn't do that without my degree, I'd discovered crime-scene cleaning. It was where I'd gotten my feet wet, so to speak. And by "wet," I didn't mean with blood and bodily fluids.

It was just a figure of speech . . . mostly.

"Do you think blood spatter could have gotten in this return vent?" Clarice pointed to the grate on the floor in front of her.

"You should check it, just in case." It always paid to be thorough.

Clarice made a face before pulling it up. As she did, she sprayed some solution inside, took a rag, and began to wipe it out.

"Hey, Gabby." Clarice's voice climbed with what sounded like confusion.

"Yes?" I braced myself for more of her questions. What would it be this time? We'd covered movies, our favorite coffee drinks, her love life, my job, and even jingles.

"I think there's something in here."

My shoulders tightened. "Like what?"

*Dust. Let it be a huge ball of dust.* I'd even settle for a cockroach or dead mouse at this point.

Based on the catch to her voice, I had a feeling that wasn't what it was.

Clarice reached inside and raised her gloved hand, revealing what she'd found.

It was a gun.

---

After Clarice showed me what she discovered, I bagged the weapon and then began to pace the room.

Could that gun have been the murder weapon?

I hadn't told the complete truth when I told her I didn't know much about what happened at the house. I'd researched the case before I came. It's what I had *always* done, and I couldn't seem to stop myself.

The victim's name was Regina Black. She was sixty-six years old. She'd retired from banking and had been widowed four years ago. Her husband had worked in finance, and the two of them appeared to be well-off.

I was basing that on the fact that historic homes in this neighborhood went for six hundred thousand and up, as well as my observation that all her furnishings were top of the line.

From what I'd researched online about this crime,

cops hadn't found the murder weapon. They assumed the killer had left with it.

So what about the gun Clarice had found? Was it the murder weapon?

But that wouldn't make any sense. Why would the person responsible shoot this woman and then hide the weapon where it could be found and traced back to him or her?

He wouldn't. It was too risky.

So what if Regina had hidden a weapon in the vent herself? What if she didn't have a gun cabinet and felt like the vent was a safe hiding spot where no one would find it?

I shook my head. What sense did that make?

None.

But that was the problem. No matter which way I looked at this, the whole thing didn't make any sense.

"What are you thinking, Gabby?" Clarice watched me as I paced.

"I'm still sorting out my thoughts, getting them in Do-Re-Mi order." *Do-Re-Mi order*? I wasn't even sure where that came from. Sometimes when I got nervous, weird stuff left my lips without any forewarning.

I thought I'd moved on from that, but obviously I hadn't. Sometimes I just hid it better than others.

"Shouldn't we call the police?" Clarice frowned as if her earlier nonstop talkativeness had been replaced with nonstop anxiety. "What if they missed this?"

"We should probably let somebody know. I mean, it only makes sense."

"You're the professional. You tell me." She narrowed her eyes. "Why do I feel like you're kind of freaking out on me right now?"

I didn't want to tell Clarice the thoughts that brewed in the back of my head. To say them out loud would sound absurd.

Besides, Clarice looked up to me. Like she'd just said, she thought of me as a professional. If I shared my theory with her, she'd lose all respect.

Before I could figure out what to say, Clarice sniffed the air. "Do you smell what I smell?"

"I don't think that's how the song goes—unless you're trying to create a new jingle or something."

"No, not the song. Like, in real life. Do you smell that?"

I took a big whiff also, and, as I did, my stomach sank.

I *did* smell something.

Smoke.

The theory I hadn't dared to voice aloud yet seemed more and more likely.

I sprang into action, knowing we probably didn't have any time to waste. "Let's grab that gun and get out of here. Now."

Her eyes widened. "It's just someone burning leaves, right?"

I shook my head. "The house is on fire."

"How do you know that?"

"Experience." This whole thing strangely mirrored the very first crime scene where I'd found evidence the police had missed. A chill went through me at the thought. "Let's get out of here. Now."

Click here to continue reading.

# ALSO BY CHRISTY BARRITT:

# BOOKS IN THE SQUEAKY CLEAN UNIVERSE

On her way to completing a degree in forensic science, Gabby St. Claire drops out of school and starts her own crime-scene cleaning business. When a routine cleaning job uncovers a murder weapon the police overlooked, she realizes that the wrong person is in jail. She also realizes that crime scene cleaning might be the perfect career for utilizing her investigative skills.

# ABOUT THE AUTHOR

*USA Today* has called Christy Barritt's books "scary, funny, passionate, and quirky."

Christy writes both mystery and romantic suspense novels that are clean with underlying messages of faith. Her books have sold more than three million copies and have won the Daphne du Maurier Award for Excellence in Suspense and Mystery, have been twice nominated for the Romantic Times Reviewers' Choice Award, and have finaled for both a Carol Award and Foreword Magazine's Book of the Year.

She is married to her Prince Charming, a man who thinks she's hilarious—but only when she's not trying to be. Christy is a self-proclaimed klutz, an avid music lover who's known for spontaneously bursting into song, and a road trip aficionado.

When she's not working or spending time with her family, she enjoys singing, playing the guitar, and exploring small, unsuspecting towns where people have no idea how accident-prone she is.

Find Christy online at:
**www.christybarritt.com**
**www.facebook.com/christybarritt**
**www.twitter.com/cbarritt**

Sign up for Christy's newsletter to get information on all of her latest releases here: **www.christybarritt.com/news letter-sign-up/**

facebook.com / AuthorChristyBarritt
twitter.com / christybarritt
instagram.com / cebarritt

Made in the USA
Middletown, DE
28 March 2024

52225357R00175